T0062980

Beyond All Flaws

Beyond All Flaws

*"They came like
whispers in the dark,
beckoning us to
come closer
and unlike the others,
we obeyed."*

• • •

CARLIN PHILIP

PARTRIDGE

A Penguin Random House Company

Library of Congress Control Number: 2015944899
ISBN: Softcover   978-1-4828-3235-8
               eBook   978-1-4828-3236-5

Print information available on the last page.

To order additional copies of this book, contact
Toll Free 800 101 2657 (Singapore)
Toll Free 1 800 81 7340 (Malaysia)
orders.singapore@partridgepublishing.com

www.partridgepublishing.com/singapore

Dedicated to my parents for supporting me all the way and to Bibin Philip, my brother for showing me the brighter side of life.

Chapter 1

Carmen is Bored

"It is the moment when the bridegroom kisses the bride," Grant used to say, a smile uplifting his stern face, *"and when confetti falls on the floor, you feel this bubbling in the pit of your stomach. It is that feeling that leaves you ensured that yes, this couple is meant to be. Weddings, dear Carmen, have the best aura. There's always the aura of hope, love and happiness. No one cares about their awful job or their meagre salaries or anything of that sort. They all drown in the happiness of the new couple. It is hard to find a hard face during any wedding. Everyone just soaks in the happiness. Weddings, dear Carmen, are divine."*

Carmen clicks her tongue in annoyance. She strongly disagrees with her father. Wedding are not her cup of tea. Especially Uncle Joe's wedding.

Of course, she had expected this. She knew that the wedding would consist of middle aged women who loved to gossip and middle aged men who loved to talk about business but she had shrugged it off. Finally, her uncle was getting married to the love of his life. So, who cares about the boring ambience, right?

Wrong.

It mattered a *lot,* actually. She thanks herself for bringing Adrian along. She's sure that if he was not there, she'd be drooling on the table.

Seated at a circular table with her best friend, she sips her wine. Lucia's recounting the story of how she and Joe met for the umpteenth time. It's getting on Carmen's nerves because she knows the story like she knows the back of her hand. From how he spilt coffee on Lucia's expensive coat to how he proposed to her in Paris.

And to add on to her list of boredom, everyone's dancing. It reminds Carmen of her single status and she feels lonelier. Plus, Uncle Joe (being the idiot that he is) invited his ex who is currently glaring at Lucia and it's freaking the shit out of Carmen because she keeps eyeing the knife that's placed near the wedding cake.

The wedding is set in a beach in and everything about the mood is romantic. With the sound of the waves hitting the rocks and soothing music, the wedding looks peaceful (ignoring the drunken men who are clearly lightweights).

Carmen stares at the vase of lilacs situated on the centre of their table. She blinks many times, steering her attention away from the vase when she hears someone clearing their throat. She tilts her head to the side and politely smiles at the waiter and nods. He places her fifth — *sixth* wine glass on the table with a weary look. She rolls her eyes and takes a sip of white wine, letting out a contented sigh.

Ah, bliss.

"You've been drinking a lot of that, don't you think?" asks Adrian raising an eyebrow. His brown mess of curls bounces as he talks and his green eyes glint with amusement. "You look nice," says Adrian taking a sip of wine from Carmen's glass and ignoring her glare, he adds, "for a change."

Carmen chuckles and slaps his shoulder playfully. She secures a strand of her auburn hair under a hairpin and lets out a discreet yawn. Adrian snickers and says, "Clearly, you're enjoying my company."

"Well, if you'd stop staring at women's butts and actually talked to me, I'd be more enthusiastic."

"Do I sense a bit of jealousy there?"

"Ah yes. Totally. I'm *fuming* with jealousy, Adrian."

"I *knew* you had a thing for me but it's nothing new. Don't worry"— he flicks a curl from his forehead— "I won't hold it against you."

"Thank God," she says melodramatically.

"But look on the bright side! We'll be leaving tomorrow!"

Her pale blue eyes twinkle at his enthusiasm. Sadly, it wasn't mutual. "Yay?" she says wearisomely.

Adrian gapes at her unbelievingly. "Are you kidding me right now? You were the one jumping down my bones the whole summer because of college. Don't start now."

She fakes an overly excited grin and squeals, "I'm *so* excited!" Dropping the grin and giving him a blank look, she asks him, "better?"

"*Much* better."

They had been friends ever since they were eleven years old. Uncle Joe and she had stepped into Valley Town with heavy hearts. Moving houses was a tedious task and the reason wasn't so light heartened at all. Nevertheless, Carmen had made her first batch of chocolate chip cookies and walked over to their neighbour's red house. She knocked on the door and she felt like they could hear how nervous she way by the way she knocked. The door flung open and an awkwardly tall boy smiled toothily at her. "Hello! You must be our neighbours!"

She doesn't remember how exactly she ended up in his attic but all she knows was that they had spent their evening talking about superheroes and she also knows that when she was going to leave, he pulled her into a hug and whispered into her ear, "We're going to be great friends."

And they did.

She sighs and listens to Adrian humming to some Frank Sinatra song that she's unaware of (he would never admit to liking Frank Sinatra songs) and taps her wine glass and tries to tune it with his humming only to have him stop and gasp.

"What on earth . . . ?"

Carmen looks at Adrian to find him gawking. She follows his gaze and ends up gawking as well because her pale blue eyes meet with striking grey ones and it mesmerizes her.

He stands three tables away from their table. She has never seen anyone with such intensity. Hot boys were a usual thing back where she lived so, she wasn't that awed when she took in his face.

His black hair is styled messily and a few strands lie on his forehead. He is tall and he looks fit and there's stubble of black beard but that's not what draws her in.

It's his eyes.

His eyes are swirling pools of gray matter. Even in a distance, she could see the tiny black specks in them and she looks away quickly because when her bright blue eyes met his gray ones, she felt like it pierced through her soul.

"Wow," she whispers hoarsely, "who is he?"

"Who knows?" mumbles Adrian taking a sip from his wine glass. He places his wine glass down and shakes his head with a disapproving frown. "I wish everyone would stop staring at him."

Carmen nods in approval. Everyone seems to have stopped their dancing just to stare at the boy. Even Rosie, her fifteen year old cousin who is blind in her right eye decided to stare at him. But Carmen would never blame them because even though she tries hard to look away, she can't. It's like his eyes are challenging her to keep staring at him.

And it's like, the more she stares at him, the more she's drawn in. She normally has a soft spot for geeky blond boys but this boy gives out an aura that orders everyone within fifteen feet to bow down and worship him.

She feels someone pat her shoulder. Without taking her eyes off him, she asks, "Yes, Adrian?"

"Remember when I told you that everyone should stop staring at the poor guy?"

"Hm."

"That stands for you too."

She blushes beetroot red and clears her throat with an air of nonchalance. "It's rude, I get it. But you can't really blame them. I mean, he's really good looking."

Adrian frowns at her disapprovingly. "I don't appreciate your sarcasm right now, Carmen. It's really rude."

Carmen raises an eyebrow. "I'm not being sarcastic . . . ?"

Even though she isn't looking at him, she can feel him giving her an incredulous stare and she decides to ignore it. Knowing Adrian, he'd give up after two minutes. After a few minutes pass by she can still feel him staring at her and so, she looks at him, huffing angrily and spits, "What?"

"I was just testing to see if you were being sarcastic with me."

"I'm not."

Adrian opens his mouth and closes it. Once. Twice. Thrice.

"When you've decided to stop imitating a fish, you can get back to me." Carmen rolls her eyes and stands up, pushing her chair back in the process. She has decided to go ask Uncle Joe who exactly this boy is.

She finds it amusing that no one has stopped staring at him. (Except for a few polite ones who have decided to swap staring for peeking.) She's also disturbed by how she finds them giving him a stink eye which is funny because according to her, it's impossible for anyone to give that boy a stink eye and it seems as though the boy was oblivious to it all.

Before she can move forward, she's pulled back by Adrian who smiles apologetically. "That was pretty rude of me but the thing is . . . I haven't seen anyone looking so ug — I mean, bad as he is."

It's Carmen's turn to imitate a fish now because as soon as he said that, she's aware of the whispers going around about how ugly the boy looked which makes her wonder if it's April Fools today.

"Say what?"

Adrian motions her to sit down and she flattens out her white dress before doing so. She props her chin on the heel of her palm and leans forward (a position which most girls would kill for) and asks, "Well?"

"The fact that you don't find him looking ug — bad is really funny. Either you're blind or you're fooling around."

There's a thing about Adrian that Carmen wishes everyone knew. Adrian is very good in convincing people. Damn good but Carmen had learnt how the twitch in his eye was a giveaway. But his eyes aren't twitching and there are no traces of mirth on his face and so, Carmen frowns. "What do you mean? He's not ugly, Adrian. Stop fooling around."

"I'm not Carmen. I'm serious and everyone else thinks so too! I just wish that they could be a bit quiet with their . . . um, observations."

She knew that. She was not oblivious to the loud whispers.

"Oh my, look at that boy! He looks awful!"

"Doesn't he?"

"My word, he's ugly!"

Carmen's mouth feels dry and so, she takes another sip of wine, relishing the tangy taste. "I . . . I don't think so."

"No shit," sighs Adrian. "He's really tall but his hair's white. Really white and his eyes are so dark. They're so dark that it looks freaking weird on his pale face. I mean, I'm just giving you small details. There's just something about him that gives off this negative vibe. God, he's ug-horrible."

• • •

"So, Carmen. Where will you be going for college?"

Carmen smiles tightly at Adrian's aunt, Gladys. She had lost count of how many times their relatives had asked her which college she was going to.

"Berkley, Ma'am," she said politely, "though Adrian—"

"—will be going to Clifford!" she squealed. "It's so romantic that you two are staying together!"

"Err . . . about that —"

"I *always* had a soft spot for childhood love stories."

"But we're just friends!"

Adrian had once suggested that she could record her denial about them being lovers and whenever she was questioned, she could just play the recording and now, Carmen seriously considered the thought.

Gladys rolls her eyes at Carmen's indignant reply. Carmen ignores her and excuses herself from the table. Uncle Joe had told her to 'socialize' and Carmen hated socializing but nevertheless, she forced herself to go through countless remarks about her and Adrian being a cute couple and how they looked perfect.

Carmen silently laughs at the thought. They were opposites and she strongly disbelieves in the 'opposites attract' theory. The only similarity that the both of them had was the fact that both of them were emotionally scarred.

When the time came for Uncle Joe and Lucia to leave in their limousine, everyone crowded around the couple. Uncle Joe was in his early forties and so was Lucia but Lucia, according to Carmen, looked like a model. She was slim and her legs . . . *oh God*, her legs. She sends Adrian a discreet wink because she knows that he, like her is thinking about the conversation that happened two years ago.

Joe: "So, uh, I met this lady today."

Carmen: "How interesting."

Joe: "Stop mocking me, Car. She's sexy.

Adrian: "How old?"

Joe: "Don't know. She looks like she's in her late thirties, though."

Adrian: "And?"

Carmen:

Adrian:

Joe: *"She's got really sexy legs!"*

Carmen: "I knew you had a leg fetish."

Joe: "I do not! You can see for yourself tomorrow."

And as much as she had protested, at the end she agreed. So, that Sunday, Adrian, Uncle Joe and her decided to stalk Lucia who worked as a primary teacher and Carmen saw for herself. In fact, when she first saw Lucia, she started questioning her heterosexuality.

Uncle Joe is flabby. He's got a double chin and a small beard forming. He and Lucia looked weird together. A complete contrast.

Uncle Joe's blue eyes meet hers and he offers her a short smile. As everyone continues to clap and laugh, Carmen gives her uncle a wavering smile, tears forming at the corner of her eyes. She raises her hand and waves at him to which he winks. Lucia gives her a reassuring smile which is synonymous to "don't worry; I'll take care of this weirdo."

The newlywed couple gets into their limousine and she feel Adrian's fingers slip through hers and she clenches it tightly. The striking realization that she would no longer wake up to Uncle Joe's delicious breakfast and his constant moans about not being handsome and his tiresome resolutions of dieting never really occurred to her until now.

"Hey. You'll be okay," says Adrian, smiling softly. "Come on, let's go."

She nods, wiping away her tears and just before she turns around, she catches a glimpse of those grey piercing eyes and that's when she freezes because she spots his eyes on her.

She feels nervous.

He's closer now and she feels this sudden urge to bow her head down. The power that was emanating from him felt warm. She gulps and finds her legs moving on their own accord.

Towards him.

She feels like she's waking in a trance. She mutters a few 'excuse me's and gently pushes a few stubborn ones until she finds herself before him.

He's surprised, she notes. His eyebrows rise up and his eyes narrow dubiously. She rubs her sweaty palms against her dress and nibbles on her lower lip, contemplating on what to say.

She settles down with a simple hello.

He blinks, looking surprised as though he was expecting a slap or a scream. He clears his throat and asks, "What part of America is this?"

Her throat feels dry and she coughs a few times. Her face feels hot and sweaty. "I'm sorry?"

"*Which part of America is this?*" he says slowly, his eyes looking meticulous as ever.

"Uh . . . C—California."

She wants to be angry, she really wants to but she *can't*. She's amused more than angry.

"Ca—what?"

"*Cali—forn—ia,*" she says slowly and even considers spelling it out to him.

"That's a strange word."

Carmen duly notes that his accent is British and it sounds perfect. Too perfect.

"It's very hot in here," he says, loosening his tie a little. Carmen can't help but raise an eyebrow at him. She's flattered that he's trying to flirt with her – or is he? Giving him a short smile, she replies, "Yeah, California has really hot summers."

Silence settles between them and she feels a few eyes burning through the back of her head. She's sure that Adrian would be one of them but she ignores them. Or at least tries to. She clears her throat and asks, "You're not from around here, are you?"

He screws his eyebrows together. "Huh, no. Where was I the last time? Syd – no. Err . . . London! Yeah, London," he grins.

Now, look. Carmen's not trying to be theatrical in any way but his grin really makes her heart skip a beat. His face lights up like a Christmas tree and she can't help but grin back at him, ignoring his absurd answers.

"So, um, how do you know Uncle Joe?"

"Joe who?"

"Joseph Barrington . . . ?"

"Oh. *Him.* Uh, my father knew him?"

She feels a tad bit cautious but she pushes that feeling away. "Do you think I look ugly?" he asks.

She lets out a nervous laugh and blurts out, "No actually. You look really hot, to be honest."

He raises his eyebrow. "Hot? How do I look *hot*? Is that possible? How does someone look hot?"

". . ."

"Must be because of the temperature, eh?" he cracks a short smile. She's almost blinded by the whiteness of his teeth.

Now, she feels angry. She feels like an idiot. He's obviously mocking her. How could she not notice that? So, she tightens her jaw and gives him a tight smile. "Maybe."

When he doesn't respond, she coughs and says, "Well, I'll see you around."

"Huh? How do you see me *around*? Is that possible?" he asks, cocking his head, curiosity swirling around his grey eyes.

"What's your name?" she asks rudely.

"Jeroën Jarvis," he says immediately.

"Carmen Collins," she says extending out her hand. He looks at her skinny arm as though observing a rare specimen and shrugs. "Okay." He gives her a short nod and turns around. Giving her another glance, he walks towards the beach, ignoring all the appalled looks.

She looks down at her arm that had been ignored and lets it fall by her side. Scowling inwardly, she turns around and walks towards Adrian who was smiling politely and talking with a couple. She joins him and smiles politely at the old couple as they averted their gaze from Adrian to her.

"Oh, Carmen," Adrian smiles, "this is Uncle Richard. My—"

"Steven's brother," she smiles brightly and shakes Richard's hand. "It's nice to finally meet you."

Richard smiles tautly. "I could say the same. Anyways, we have to rush. I'll see you two later. Where are you guys heading to for college?"

"California," they reply in unison. Richard nods and straightens his black coat. "Well, then. I'll see you around."

They smile and nod, knowing that they wouldn't. After the couple leaves, Adrian glares at Carmen and asks, "What were you and that guy talking about?"

Carmen sighs and twirls a strand of her red hair and says, "Not much."

"It didn't look like that."

"I'll tell you later, okay?" She says. Adrian nods reluctantly and says, "Well, let's go. Everyone's leaving."

Before slipping her hand into Adrian's, she turns around and looks for Jeroën but she doesn't see him. Instead, she sees people smiling at her. Smiling back at them, she slips her hand into Adrian's warm hand and wishes for nothing more than to never see him again.

Never to see Jeroën Jarvis ever again.

• • •

Chapter 2

Adrian was a Fragile Kid

When boys preferred to pick up fights, sleep around with girls, smoke and do drugs, Adrian preferred counting the stars, watching sunsets and staring at *her* photo. But *that* never stopped him from becoming the popular guy. He was loved by all. Parents would point at him and tell their sons to be like him. Girls would sigh dreamily and say that he was the one.

All he had to do was put on a mask that smiled all the time.

And he wouldn't lie if you ever asked him if he was suicidal but when he grew up, met new people, got out of his shell; he realized that he wanted to live. He wanted to escape. He wanted to *breathe* freely without having the memories of his past haunt him forever. Adrian felt like he was in this . . . metaphorical bubble of existence and he was clueless as to how he got there or how to get *out* of there. He knew that just a single *pop* would mark his downfall.

Of course, Adrian always believed that all bad things would come to an end and his hope came in the form of a parentless girl who had stood on his porch with a jar of cookies. Carmen.

She was the only one who knew how he loved to chase the sun away and how he cowered in fear when the moon arrived because the moon always bought his demons along and she was the only one there to protect him. Adrian could be himself—without the protection of his mask in front of Carmen.

Which was why, when Adrian's dad, Steven had asked him if he wanted to stay alone in an apartment for college, Adrian replied a firm and resolute "no" because he could not survive and fend off his demons without her.

Staring at their apartment in awe, he smiles. He sneaks a discreet look at his best friend whose mouth was slightly ajar as she took in their apartment. She squeals in a very non-Carmen way and grips his hand tightly, skipping about in their living room. "Dude, it's so spacious!"

Steven O'Connor studies the living room in different angles. First, he sits down on the window seat and inspects the room. Then, he walks to the kitchen door and looks around again.

"Done with your observations, dad?" Adrian asks, a sly smile playing around his lips because he knows that his dad dislikes the fact that his son is living far away from him.

". . . Yeah," his dad says shrugging. "You guys want me to help you unpack?"

Carmen shakes her head. "Nada. We just have to unpack our clothes and a few belongings. Thank God it comes furnished."

"Yeah, yeah," says Steven and clears his throat. "I need to talk to both of you. Have a seat."

Adrian rolls his eyes because he knows what's coming. He walks lazily towards the red love seat (which he has already planned on throwing out after his father leaves). Carmen shrugs and joins Adrian. She props her chin on the heel of her palm, and asks, "What's up?"

"Now, I know you guys are really excited for college and all that but hum, just before I leave, I should tell you two something"— he leans forward like he's going to tell a secret —"you two must *always* and I mean *always* call us—"

"Dad!" Adrian huffs, "we know and we will! We're not kids. We're *adults!*"

"Which is what I'm worried about," mutters Steven.

Carmen giggles and shakes her head, a red fringe escaping her pony tail. "We'll call you guys. It's not like you guys won't ever come here, right?"

Adrian has this sudden urge to kick Carmen's leg for putting ideas into his dad's head but he resists. *Calm down, Adrian. Calm down.*

Steven's green eyes lighten up. "Yea, of course I'll come! And Joe will be here after his honeymoon so . . . you guys won't miss us much," he winks. "Also, both of you are responsible *adults*. You know what good and bad and—"

"Dad. Are you seriously teaching us about safe sex, right *now*?"

". . ."

It's not long before Adrian convinces his dad to leave. After unpacking their boxes and claiming their rooms, they set all their clothes up and heave a sigh of relief.

"Well, that's that," sighs Carmen, sipping on the banana milkshake that Adrian had made. "We're *finally* on our own."

"Yep," he confirms and takes a bite of his chicken sandwich. Placing his elbows on the counter, he smiles and says, "It's our ticket to start over new."

"It's *my* ticket to start over new," Carmen narrows her eyes. Finishing her milkshake, she places it in the sink and turns on the tap. Glancing at Adrian who raises his eyebrows at her, she says, "You have nothing wrong with you."

"You talk like you're abnormal," he snorts before stopping and wincing slightly knowing he hit a soft spot.

Carmen stills and sighs. She turns around and gives him a soft smile. Softly, she says, "I am."

Adrian closes his eyes wearily. She never understands. She never will. No matter how many times he's told her that she's *not*, she'd never believe him. He always tells her (and tells himself) that the two of them were *not* abnormal or weird or anything absurd.

If anything, *she* was luckier. Luckier than him. At least, she didn't have to fear the night or live with the guilt—

Stop playing the 'Who's gone through worse' game, he scolds himself.

"So!" Carmen chirps wiping her hands on a blue washcloth. "Why don't we go and visit our neighbours?"

"*Neighbours?*" he says in distaste. "I was thinking of going for grocery shopping. We hardly have any good other than junk food."

"You're the only teenage who complains about junk food," she mutters.

Adrian cups his hand over his ear and says, "What was that, Cars?"

"Nothing. How about this? Let's visit our neighbour and then go for grocery shopping."

"Fine," he sighs dejectedly. "Move your skinny butt, then," he snaps.

She gives him an amused smirk. "Should've known that your bi-polarity would come up sooner or later."

• • •

AKELARD GAVIN

"Sounds German."

"Oh great," smiles Carmen. "Another fellow German."

"You're *half* German."

Carmen rolls her eyes at him and knocks on the door. They wait for a few minutes and then look at each other. "Is he there or what?"

They hear a loud bang and an 'ouch!' The door opens slowly and a black head pops out. "Y—Yes?"

"Um . . . hi!" says Adrian peering over Carmen's shoulder to see more of the boy. He gives him a charming smile and notices a dark tinge appearing on his sunken cheeks.

"H—hi . . . ?"

"My name's Carmen and this is my friend, Adrian" —Carmen points a finger to Adrian — "and we live in the flat next to yours. We moved in this morning and we thought we'd give our neighbour a visit. Are you German? I—"

"Yeah," interrupts Adrian giving Akelard a tight smile. He knows how Carmen's rambling can get out of hand. "Can we get in?" he asks bluntly.

He ignores Carmen's glare as Akelard shuffles around and opens the door wider. "S—sure."

His apartment is clean. Period. Adrian can literally see each corner sparkle and he cannot spot a single blemish or spot of dust.

Strangely, he feels calm in Akelard's apartment. There're a lot of plants situated near the windows. He knows that Akelard has arranged his apartment with some sort of theme and according to what he saw, he smiles.

Cities.

There a huge banner with all the metropolitan cities scrawled in a very elegant handwriting. There're photos of minimalistic images of the Eiffel Tower, Leaning Tower of Pisa, you name it.

He spots a pile of books lying neatly on the black tea table. He takes one and reads out the title.

"Yo, you're a Law student?"

Akelard nods mutely. Adrian has the feeling that he's intimidating him. So, he puts on a sweet smile and says, "Really? Which college?"

"C—Clifford."

"Yeah?" hums Adrian. "What a coincidence. Me too."

"R—really?!" he squeaks and then composes himself as Carmen and Adrian shoot him *what the hell* looks. "I—I mean, c—could you d—do me a favour?"

Adrian knows what it is but he prompts him to go on. Akelard blushes at the penetrating gaze of Carmen's blue eyes. Adrian mentally rolls his eyes. Carmen had a way of scaring of people.

"C—could you d—drop me to college?"

Carmen grins widely. "Of course, he can! Hey, how about this? We're going for grocery shopping. Do you want to join us?'

Adrian pales and clenches his jaw.

Akelard grins, taking the duo by surprise.

"Well then, let's go!"

• • •

Carmen sees irritation creeping up Adrian's neck.

She feels that there's something about her neighbour. She watches how he flinches when he feels people's attention on him. She watches how he tries to zip up the zipper all the way to his lips when girls sneer at him.

"He's weird."

"Aren't we all?" she murmurs, placing a milk carton in their shopping cart and veers it forward. Her eyes skim through the different products of cheese.

"Look. Look. Carmen, *look.*"

Adrian tugs on Carmen's sleeve and she turns to see what Adrian's pointing at. He's pointing at Akelard who picks up a carton of adult pampers and drops it in his shopping cart.

They look away quickly and act as if they never saw it happen. Akelard pushes the cart towards them and Carmen can see that he's trying to hide the carton of pampers by a box of Captain Crunch.

"Well, are you done, Akelard?" Carmen smiles. Adrian can see Akelard's eye soften a bit at the sight of Carmen's smile.

"Y—yeah."

They stroll over to the checkout and Adrian starts to empty their shopping cart. Carmen has this strong urge to burst out laughing at the cashier who was trying her best to pull her shirt down. Of course, Adrian being Adrian ignores her.

Akelard moves forward, stumbling on his extra-large pants. He blushes at the incredulous stare of the cashier and starts to empty his cart. As soon as he gives the adult pampers to the cashier, she snorts.

"Wow. This is hilarious. *Adult pampers*, really?"

She starts to giggle and Akelard's face goes red. Carmen clears her throat and says, "You're here to do your job. Not judge your customers by what they buy. Who's your manager?"

The cashier widens her eyes. "I—I'm sorry. You don't have to—"

"Just hurry *up*, for God sakes," huffs Adrian. "There're people waiting, you know?"

• • •

"Well, this was nice," says Carmen. "College starts at nine for both of you right?"

They nod.

"Great. Mine starts at eight and it's twelve, now. Plus, Adrian has to drop me and I need my beauty sleep—"

"Th—Thank you," says Akelard softly.

"S'okay," yawns Adrian. "Well, we better get going. See you tomorrow, Akelard."

Akelard widens his eyes and nods frantically before fumbling with his keys and he opens his door. "Y—you guys want c—coffee or something?"

"It's midnight," Adrian deadpans.

"Right," he mumbles.

Carmen chuckles and says, "You're cute. Let's go, Adrian. Good night, Akelard."

"G—Good night."

They walk up to their flat and Adrian pushes Carmen as soon as she unlocks the door.

"Hey!"

"I'm sleepy." He kicks off his shoes and pulls of his jacket and throws it across their lounge. "Weird guy, eh?"

"Yeah. He's nice, though. Well, I'm off to sleep and you should be too. My college starts an hour earlier than yours."

He nods and says "good night" before she leaves and settles down for a bottle of water to quench his thirst. After that, he switches off the light in the kitchen and enters his bedroom before slipping off his socks. He rubs his weary eyes and settles down into his pyjamas.

This time, like all times, he prays to God that this night would be different before shutting his eyes. But it never does.

"You killed me. You killed me. I had dreams, son. So many dreams but you ruined it all. We could've been a happy family. We could've been everything you ever wanted . . ."

"Stop."

"You could've stopped them. You were just a boy. Which ten year old would kill his mother?"

"I'm sorry. Please . . ."

Why? Why? You're a murderer. A ruthless murderer . . ."

"No . . ."

"Murderer. Dare you to deny it, son. Murderer. Mur—"

"NO!"

Adrian sits up, his eyes wide and perspiration forming on his forehead. He brushes off the sweat with his sleeve of his pyjamas. "I'm not a murderer," he mutters. "I'm not a murderer," he sobs, silently at first. After a minute, it gets louder and louder until—

"Adrian?"

He feels the edge of his bed sink deeper and soon, a fresh smell of jasmines engulfs him. "Adrian, come on."

"They never stop!" he yells, looking at those bright blue eyes and then says softly, "they just . . . never stop . . ."

"Adrian—"

"I'm not a murderer, Cars. I swear to God, I'm not," he gulps. "I'm not."

"I know you're not," she sighs. "Come on," she says, pulling him by his elbow. "You can swallow your pride and come and sleep with me."

He cracks a smile, his face wet with tears and says, "I always knew you had a thing for me."

"Yeah, yeah," Carmen rolls her eyes. "Are you coming or what?"

"I'm coming, you needy girl."

"Keep talking. Do you know that I know your password for Facebook?"

". . . So?"

"It just takes one second for me to post that picture of you sucking your thumb with Tom & Jerry boxers, hun."

His face pales. "You told me you deleted that!"

"Yeah. Well, what can I say? I'm a good liar."

He rolls his eyes at her with a small smile playing on his lips. Before slipping into the jasmine smelling covers of Carmen he prays again, like every night.

He prays for a chance to be like Carmen.

Fearless.

• • •

Chapter 3

Carmen is Devoid of Fear

According to Carmen, fear was some sort of feeling that gave meaning to people's life. Everyone's afraid of *something* and that something motivates one to move forward.

Everyone except Carmen.

As a child, she never experienced fear. That kind of bubbling in the pit of your stomach or adrenaline rushing down your veins or goose bumps crawling up your skin — she never understood that and she still doesn't.

She just doesn't get it.

She always felt like she was dead on the inside because she had no control of her flaw. Absolutely none. If she did have, she would've changed it because she wanted to have that *excitement* and *thrill* of living more than anything in this world.

Standing in the midst of students rushing around to get to their first class in time, she wishes to feel that enthusiasm. That eagerness to study.

She feels nothing.

After admiring the tall structures of her college and trying to digest the fact that she's actually in college and she's going to be an architect, she sighs to herself. She pushes back her red hair and pulls on the lapels of her blue blazer. She shakes her head to get rid of her cynical thoughts and walks up the stairs to her first lecture: Physics.

When she enters the room, she bites her lip in annoyance. She's late and she hates being late. The professor pauses at her untimely entrance. He's explaining something that looks foreign to her. He purses her lips and motions her to go and take a seat.

She smiles back politely and walks hastily to the back of the lecture theatre. There are plenty of empty seats but she loves sitting at the back. Muttering a lot of 'excuse me' and 'sorry, I didn't see your leg' and 'your bag's in the way', she plops down on a red cushioned seat next to a boy who smiles politely at her.

She smiled back and sets her bag down. Retrieving her black notebook, she sneaks a look at the notebook of the boy next to her. There're plenty of diagrams and elegant doodles of mathematical formulas that look anything but familiar to her. Carmen sighs again. The boy looks at her and smiles.

"I can give you my book after this class," he says and quickly adds, "if you want."

She grins widely. "I'd love that. Thanks! My name's Carmen."

He sneaks a look at the professor and says, "Omar. Omar Abbas."

So, after their Physics class Omar and Carmen head to the cafeteria. He gives her his book and invites her to eat breakfast with his girlfriend. He won't stop talking about her and as he keeps babbling about his girlfriend, Carmen observes him. She notes that his eyes are a bright blue and his hair is neatly combed to the side. He's tanned and he has a bit of Scottish accent which sounds just right.

"Hey, Carmen?"

She blinks and smiles, "Yeah?"

His brown eyes glint with amusement. "The cafeteria's that way—" he flicks his thumb to the side "—you're heading to Geometry class. Are you that eager?"

Carmen chuckles and says, "Nope. Come on."

They walk out of the building and spot their cafeteria. People are seated in circles, laughing and eating their food. She smiles. Unlike High school, right now, she couldn't differentiate between the nerds or the geeks, the jocks or the popular and the weirdoes or the freaks.

Omar heads to a table in the corner of their cafeteria and Carmen spots a brunette girl talking on her phone. Omar pulls out a chair and gestures Carmen to sit down. The girl on the phone sees Carmen and immediately puts her phone down.

"Lay, this is Carmen. Carmen, this is Layla."

Carmen smiles at her. "Hey."

"Hi!" she chirps. "It's funny that Omar's bring you here. The idiot rarely shows me his friends."

Carmen chuckles. "Well, I'm in his Physics class."

"That's cool," she pouts. "The only class I have with him is CAD."

"Would you like something to eat, Carmen?" asks Omar, standing up. "I'm going to get my food."

"Oh, no. It's—"

"No, it's fine. I'll get it. I like being a gentleman, anyways." He smirks at Layla who rolls her eyes

"I thought chivalry was long dead."

"Well," he says. "I bought it back. What do you want?"

"Uh, a burger and soda would do fine. Here"—Carmen hands him some change— "call me if you need more."

"Okay."

They stare at each other for a few minutes until Omar breaks the silence. "What? Did you expect me to go all like 'Oh no! It's fine! I'll use my money'? Well, sorry," he smiles sheepishly.

"Omar!" scolds Layla. "Just buy it for her!"

"Gosh, no," Carmen laughs. "Don't do that. If there's extra money, buy a packet of skittles?"

"Bingo."

When he leaves, Layla leans closer, her brown bangs covering her light brown eyes. "So, Carmen. Where do you stay?"

"Um, Red Hill apartments? I live there with my best friend."

"Awesome! We live a few streets away from there. Show me your schedule."

After comparing their schedules, Carmen finds out that they have English as a common subject. Carmen noticed that Layla was a very bubbly girl and she liked that a lot. She was sensible and polite and never peered too much into Carmen's personal life.

"Here you go," huffs Omar, pushing her tray towards her. "The queue over there's crazy."

Omar gives Layla a peck on her cheek before shoving fries into his mouth. Carmen bites her lip to stop laughter from spilling out as she notes two red spots appearing on Layla's cheeks.

"Ow!" groans Omar as Layla slaps his shoulder. "What was that for?"

"For hogging like a pig. Can't you see two ladies sitting with you?"

"I only see one," he mutters, glancing at Carmen. "Can't find another."

Carmen smiles softly as the couple start bickering. They looked cute together and most of all, they looked happy too.

When the bell rings, she leaves with the pair thinking that it would be nice to fall in love.

• • •

"Excuse me?"

The boy pushes his glasses up and frowns. "Yes?"

"Do you know where the CAD class is? My schedule seems to have it wrong—"

"It's in Room 23." He frowns. "Now, stop bothering me."

Carmen clenches her jaw and takes a look at her watch. Its 8:50 and Adrian would probably leave ten minutes later. She walks down the hallways and enters her CAD class.

Unlike most of her lecture theatres, her CAD class was a regular class with two computers on each table. She walks to the third row and sits down, placing her back on her lap. Momentarily, students start filling the room and as usual, no one sits with Carmen.

Her professor, a short woman with a turquoise sweat and a matching skirt, enters the class. Nobody notices her until she taps the board three times.

"Well, good morning. My name's Michelle Brown and I'll be teaching you CAD for this semester. And," continues Michelle, "I don't like starting my class with a bunch of strangers. So, you will start by introducing yourselves."

Carmen cracks a smile as she hears loud groans and protests.

"We're in college! Give us a break, would you?"

"We're not in High school! We're way past that!"

"Oh c'mon!"

The door opens with a loud groan and everybody stills. Even Carmen.

"May I come in?"

Carmen hears a book drop and a small squeal. She turns toward the door and does a double take.

Jeroën Jarvis.

Her professor, Michelle Brown's face turns white and so does everyone around her. She doesn't miss the looks of disgust they throw him. Everyone shifts uncomfortably in their chairs.

Everyone except Carmen.

She's drooling. Not literally, *of course.* But she's enticed by this . . . powerful aura that he emanates and she can't stop but wonder *who* exactly he is.

"W—what's your n—name?" stammers Michelle, her face paling deeply and Carmen almost doubts that if Jeroën takes a step closer towards her, she would faint.

"Jeroën Jarvis," he grins, gums and all. Everyone cringes at the sight of his smile while Carmen (on the other hand) melts on the inside.

"T—take a seat, please . . .?"

"Sure," he says and surveys the rom. Carmen mentally does a victory dance as she realises that the only empty seat was right next to her. His eyes land on the empty chair right next to her and his eyes drift to her. She inhales a sharp intake of breath as his grey eyes stare right at her. There's a small quirk in his lips as he strolls lazily towards her.

She finds it disturbing when people inch away from him in disgust when it was the exact opposite of what she would do.

As he slides into his chair, she finds herself unconsciously adjusting her messy hair. She had planned on tying her red hair into a ponytail but since Adrian always said that she looked better with her hair down, she decided to go with her hair down on her first day of college.

No one talks after that. Michelle hurriedly wipes her face with her handkerchief and when she speaks, her voice shivers.

Is this all happening because of Jeroën Jarvis?

• • •

He knocks on his door three times.

Sticking his hands in his pockets, Adrian flicks a curl from his forehead. He hears a lot of shuffling around and then, the door opens. He smiles at Akelard who smiles shyly at him. He's wearing a white button down shirt with black pants.

"Ready to go?"

"Y—yeah. Um . . . do you want some coffee?"

He chuckles. "No, Akelard. I'm great. Come on."

Akelard steps out of his flat and tries to lock the door but his hands are shivering way too much. Adrian cocks an eyebrow and says, "You want some help, bud?"

"N—no, I can do it!" he laughs, almost nervously. "I—It's just very cold."

"Cold?" he asks incredulously. He's sweating even when the air conditioner is on in his room. "Just give me the keys," he says and not waiting for an answer, he grabs the keys and locks the door with ease.

"There you go," he smiles, looking at Akelard who is intent on avoiding Adrian's gaze. "C'mon," he mutters, skipping down the stairs and stops. "You can take the lift, if you want. I'm just . . . used to taking the stairs is all."

If anything, he had expected Akelard to blush and run off to the lift. He *never* expected Akelard to *smirk* at him.

Akelard Gavin smirked at him.

"Sure," he chuckled. Glancing up at Adrian, he asks, "what?"

"You didn't stutter."

"W—well, I—I—"

"Okay," he says flatly. "Let's get going."

• • •

Clifford.

Ever since, he had the dream of becoming a lawyer, Clifford was all he could think about. He just couldn't take his eyes or head off the tall and titanic structures and the greenery. Everything looked just right.

"Hey, Akelard?" Adrian says, parking his Toyota Prius near a Maserati. He didn't feel ashamed of parking a Toyota Prius in the midst of expensive cars. He always felt like home in his car.

"Y—yeah?'

"You ready, bud?" he cracks a smile, loosening his seatbelt.

"Yeah."

But Akelard looked anything but enthusiastic.

• • •

"Hey!" shouts Adrian trying to get the attention of a certain black headed boy. Girls give him flattering looks while the boys shoot him annoyed looks but Adrian shrugs it off. He's almost used to it.

Almost used to the fact that people loved this fake side more than who he really was.

"Akelard!" he yells again. This time, Akelard looks at him and gives him a million dollar smile. He tries to squeeze himself through the crowd of people who rushed towards the exit of the college. Adrian considers helping him out but before he can move a step, Akelard's out of the crowd and he's gasping.

"What took you so long?" he asked as they walked towards his car. "Classes got over half an hour earlier."

"I got caught up," he rushes and wipes off the sweat tricking down his jaw. Adrian unlocks his car and gets in, shutting the door after him. Taking a look at his watch, he says, "Carmen must be at home by now. Hurry up."

As soon as Akelard shuts the door and snaps his seat belt, Adrian veers his car out of the parking lot.

"H—hey, Adrian?"

"Yeah?"

"Did you h—hear about Sh—Sheila David?"

"Uh, no," he hums, stopping at a red signal. "Who's that?"

"A g—girl."

"No shit, Sherlock."

"N—no, I mean, she's really beautiful and eve—everyone's sort of following her. I saw h—her." Akelard smiles as though he won an Oscar. "She's r—really beautiful. Haven't s—se—"

"Seen?" helps Adrian.

"Yeah," Akelard blushes. "I haven't seen anyone like her. She's every kind too."

"You like her?"

"What?!" he shrieked, his face flooding red. "Of course not!"

"Okay, okay," chuckles Adrian. "She sounds like a dream, though."

• • •

Chapter 4

Adrian is Starstruck

Earlier when Akelard offered to buy Adrian a bagel from their cafeteria before they go for their classes, Adrian had agreed.

Their cafeteria—unlike his expectations, was by far the best cafeteria. They gave steaming hot coffee that made Adrian curl his toes and sigh in bliss.

Right *now*, though, it isn't the coffee or the toasted bagel that makes him gape in wonder.

It's Sheila David.

She's sitting under a mahogany tree. Her legs are stretched out and her blonde hair is tied up in a French ponytail. She's reading a book and Adrian wants her to look up because he desperately wants to see her eyes. *She* gave off an aura of omniscience and elegance.

Akelard's description of Sheila did her no justice.

"Le—let's go?" asks Akelard, biting his bagel. "Wh—oh."

Adrian can feel Akelard grinning at him Adrian just *can't* take his eyes off of her and what's even amusing is that he's not the only one staring at her. Almost everyone around her is staring at her.

So, instead of following the norm of staring at her, Adrian decides to talk to her. Sending a tight lipped smile to Akelard, he sticks his hands into his pockets, runs his hands through his curly hair and smiles his million dollar smile.

Ignoring the curious looks, he walks towards her, his palms awfully sweaty. He didn't quite like the effect that she was giving him. Usually, he's never so nervous when he meets girls. Right now, he feels like he's in primary school.

"Uh, excuse me?" he says, his voice slipping into a deeper octave. She looks up and Adrian stills.

Her brown eyes peer curiously at him. She cocks her head to the side and smiles, "yes?"

"Huh, hi. I'm Adrian. Adrian Mon—I mean, O'Connor." He blushes.

Her lips quirk up in amusement. "You look like you're confused with your name."

"No," he chuckles. Pointing at the empty spot of grass next to her, he asks, "Can I join you?"

She scoots a little to the side and pats the spot. Adrian grins at her and sits down, Indian style. "What's your name?" He asks.

"You don't know my name?" she asks flatly. Adrian reddens and says, "I was just trying to make conversation."

"I'll tell you a better way," she smirks. "What's your middle name?"

"Oh *no*," he chuckles. "Trust me, you wouldn't want that."

"Well, I do," she says. She closes her books and puts in on her lap. Propping her chip on the heel of her palm, she raises an eyebrow. "Well?"

"Promise me you won't judge me?"

"I won't and I won't."

He sighs. "Okay. My name's Adrian . . . Montague O'Connor."

Adrian counts to three. On cue, she bursts into a fit of laughter and he thinks that her laugh can easily lighten up anyone's dampened mood. Sobering up, she grins at him. "Your parents were huge on Romeo and Juliet?"

"My mom," he huffs. "She sort of made it like a joke because my parents met in a Romeo and Juliet play in high school."

"Aw, that's sweet," she chuckles. "Do you live here or did you move . . .?"

"Yeah. Um, I live in a town a bit near to Sacramento. I live here with my best friend."

"Must be fun, huh?"

"Oh yeah. We're independent and all that. What about you?"

She looks at him with a mysterious smile. "If I told you, you would laugh at me."

"I would?

"Pretty sure."

"Ha, I won't. Where are you from?"

Sheila's hazel brown eyes have a mysterious glint in them when she says, "don't bother. I come from a place far out of your reach."

Adrian shrugs. "Okay, then. Well, we have to go. Classes start in five minutes. What's your first class?"

"Criminology," she wrinkles her nose. "You?"

"Criminal Justice. See you later."

"Yeah, you too."

• • •

"What's wrong with him?" whispers Carmen. Akelard looks at where she's looking and laughs softly at Adrian's dazed expression. "I—I don't know."

"You sure 'bout that? It doesn't seem like that"— she takes a sip of her coffee— "and you know it." Taking a look at the clock that hung above their bookshelf, she says, "It's getting quite late."

"Y—yeah, I'll leave!" He rushes out the words and gets up from Adrian's bean bag, stumbling in the process.

"Whoa, whoa," Carmen catches his arm. "Chillax. Sorry, but you'll be stuck with us for a couple of hours."

"I—I don't w—want to bother . . ."

"You're not," she chuckles. "Why don't you switch on the TV and watch something? Adrian will be done with making dinner by then."

He nods mutely and plops down on a cushion. Carmen skips over to the counter and sits on a barstool. "Adrian?"

Adrian, who's busying himself by stirring a bowl of vegetables, murmurs, "Hm?"

"Mind telling me what happened in college today?"

Adrian stills and sneaks a look at Carmen who raises an expectant eyebrow at him. He chuckles nervously because he knows he can't get out of this easily. He wipes his greasy hands on his apron and says, "I'll tell you if you tell me why you were so disturbed earlier this evening?"

Carmen inhales a sharp breath and says, "I told you yester—"

"Is this about that Jeroën guy?" he demands. When she doesn't reply, he continues, "God, Carmen. I *told* you not to worry about—"

"I'm going mad, Adrian!" she snaps loudly. She can feel Akelard peering curiously over at the counter so she lowers her voice. "I'm going mad. You don't understand. *Everyone's* seeing him . . . I—I can't. I can't stay oblivious to all the disgusted looks and shit when I'm the *only* one who's drooling when he's around. This *can't* be normal! I—I'm tired of being weird, Adrian," she says wearily, holding her head with her hands. "I'm just tired."

"Carmen—"

"You know what? I'm going to a psychologist."

Adrian freezes. "Say what?"

"I'm going to a psychologist and I've already booked an appointment," she says, "it's in two days."

"Why didn't you tell this to me?" he scowled. "We could've talked about it!"

"And then what's going to happen? You'll disapprove of it, anyway. Forget me. What's gotten into your head? You look like you've been dreaming all this while," she chuckles.

"Oh, I haven't been dreaming," he sighs with a dazed look. "You know what? I'll tell you after Akelard's. The little minx has been eavesdropping on us."

They hear a thud, an 'ouch!' and an indignant reply "N—No, I haven't!"

• • •

"So, you're telling me that Adrian made your neighbour puke out the pasta that *he* made?"

Carmen grins at Markus and gives an affirmative nod. "You know how bad Adrian is at making pasta. Remember last year when he gave you food poisoning because of his pasta?"

Markus scowls. His image blurs for a few seconds and so is his voice. "What was that?" asks Carmen. He says something and Carmen still can't hear, so she absentmindedly replies, "Yeah totally. Anyway, he's making Akelard some soup now and Akelard doesn't really want to eat because he's scared that it might cause a reaction."

Markus' blonde hair covers his left eye as he laughs. She smiles and it almost feels nostalgic. She cracks her neck and lets out a loud yawn. "How's that girlfriend of yours—Elle, isn't it?"

"Careful there, Carmen. I can almost *feel* the jealousy."

Carmen rolls her eyes. "Well, I did date you first and she doesn't quite like me because of that."

"Oh, it's not that," he says and adds softly, "it's just . . . she feels a bit intimidated by you."

Carmen nod. "Yeah. After all, I *am* the Fearless Freak."

"Hey," he says, leaning closer. His camera wavers a bit which blurs his image but he adjusts it and continues, "Don't be too hard on yourself. She was just intimidated by your appearance."

"Is that supposed to make me feel better?" she deadpans.

"Well, I hope so," he chuckles. "You always looked weird with that red lipstick and pale skin. You looked like a witch."

"Yeah, okay. You're not really helping me."

"I'm just saying. Thank God you got rid of that lipstick."

"Well, I have to go and you should too. Have fun there," she winks.

Markus groans, "Oh God! I swear, my roommates are out and they're going to come home late and drunk. The last time, Jason almost tried to kiss me."

"He's lucky that he didn't kiss you," she smirks. "You were a lousy kisser."

"Carmen, that was in the past. Now—" he flexes his muscles "—I'm much better."

She wrinkles her nose and tucks her hair behind her ear. "Good to know. I'll be logging off now."

"Gee, if you really wanted to get rid of me, you could've just—"

Carmen Collins has logged out.

• • •

Chapter 5

Carmen is Flustered

"You do know that what you're doing is wrong, right?"

Carmen's face is red as a tomato when Jeroën leans over and types something on her computer. She always wondered why he wore full sleeved shirts and thick sweaters even when it was blazing hot. Earlier this week, people had come up to her and offered her a treat because they felt sorry as she had to be Jeroën's partner.

"Thanks," she mutters. "I don't really understand this topic."

Jeroën looks at her and as usual, she tries to look away because she feels as though his eyes are questioning her past. "Can I come with you?"

"Huh?"

"Can I come with you when you go home?"

She widens her blue eyes and chokes out, "Why?"

"Because I am lonely," he says like it's obvious enough. "And you seem like a nice person." His last statement echoes in her head like a broken record. *You seem like a nice person.*

"But . . . I hardly know you," she says.

Jeroën stares at her and this goes on for a couple of minutes. "It's not right," she says. "I mean, we don't even know each other and it's absurd to take a stranger home."

"Stranger?" he asks, cocking his head to the side. "Am I a stranger?"

He isn't and she knows that. They've been having small conversations over the week and often, she feels very safe with him. Omar and Layla have often questioned her about Jeroën and she really didn't know how to justify their relationship.

"You're not," she sighs dejectedly. "Fine. After your classes, meet me in the parking lot."

• • •

She rings the bell twice.

Carmen's fuming and she has already prepared her speech when the door opens. As if on cue, the door opens.

"Where were you?" she demands, placing her hands on her hips. "We waited for half an hour and we had to take a cab with this flirty cab driver who—"

Adrian gapes at Jeroën who stares robotically at him. "Wh—what's this guy doing here?" he says, looking mortified.

"Adrian," she says with a look that tells him to behave. "This is Jeroën. Jeroën, this is Adrian, my best friend and flat mate."

"Good evening," says Jeroën with an air of cockiness.

Adrian doesn't answer. Instead, he's shivering in fear because despite his ug —horrible appearance, he reeks of authority and power and Adrian has this sudden urge to bow down. He settles down with a glare. "Why did you bring this guy over here?"

"Don't be rude, Adrian," she says, avoiding his eyes. Nudging him aside, so that they could get in, she gestures Jeroën to get inside. When he does, she bows a little and says, "Welcome to our humble abode."

Jeroën gives her a charming smile. Carmen lets out a dreamy sigh whereas Adrian grimaces.

"Shut the door, Adrian," she says with a blank look. He glares at her and shuts the door with a bang. "You didn't answer my question. Why didn't you pick us up and what are you doing here? Don't you have afternoon classes?"

"I do," Adrian says giving Jeroën a stink eye, "and we'll be leaving shortly."

Akelard walks out of their kitchen, sipping on a strawberry shake. His eyes widen as he takes in Jeroën's appearance and lets out a little scream.

"Err . . ."

"Who—who's that?!" he yelps, hiding behind Adrian.

Carmen wishes for the ground to swallow her up because Jeroën has this amused smirk on his face. "Akelard, Jeroën's my friend and Jeroën, Akelard's my neighbour."

"Pleasure," says Jeroën with a slight nod. And that was another weird thing about Jeroën. He always talked formally.

Adrian pulls Akelard to the door and with one last glare at Carmen; he pushes Akelard out and shuts the door after him.

Carmen lets out a nervous laugh. "So, hum, that's them. What do you want to do?"

"I do not know. You tell me."

"I could make some popcorn and we could watch a movie," she says weakly.

•••

"Is that it?" he asks incredulously. "How is that a happy ending?"

"What's wrong with it?" she asks and waits for the disc to be ejected.

"What happens *after* the marriage? I have heard the worst things happen after marriage."

"Um—well, since its 'Happily Ever After', we can assume that nothing of that sort happens," she says and points at his empty cup, "you want some more beer?"

"No," he says, waving his hand. His black hair is messed up as usual, and his black leather jacket is zipped all the way to his neck. "We have watched three movies and all of them have happy endings. Is that possible? Is that why humans are more oblivious to natural catastrophes?"

"What do you mean?"

"Like . . . failure. We know that at one point of time, we will have to go through it. So, why are we afraid to go through it? Like . . . death. It is a natural occurrence. Yet, why are we afraid of it?"

"I . . . I don't know," confesses Carmen. "I guess we *choose* to remain oblivious."

"Well," he yawns, "where is your roommate? It is getting dark."

"He said something about getting his car fixed or something," she says, picking up a few popcorns that are strewn on the floor. "Do you want to watch something else?"

•••

"Wait, so are they . . . dating?" he asks. He says 'dating' like it's a foreign word.

"No," she replies politely. "They're friends . . . with benefits." She cringes as Justin Timberlake kisses Mila Kunis. She didn't feel particularly comfortable watching this movie with Jeroën but he had insisted.

"And what are the benefits?"

"Err . . . sex, I guess?"

"How is that a benefit?" he asks incredulously. "That is bloody absurd!"

• • •

"How is giving a diamond necklace to her romantic? Is that not wastage of money?"

"He's rich and all girls would love to have a diamond necklace," she replies wearily. "Must you question every single thing that happens in movies?"

"What about roses?" He demands. "Aren't those romantic?"

"I don't know, Jeroën. I guess people are bored of it."

"Wow," he mutters. "The world has *definitely* changed."

• • •

Chapter 6

Adrian's Smile Felt Like a Ton

His cheeks hurt and his grin falters as his friends leave the parking lot. He's supposed to be used to the attention he got. Boys and girls came up to him asking for him to join them in their parties.

"No," he had politely replied, "my family's here for dinner."

That's a lie, by the way. He smirks to himself and spots her. She's talking to a taxi driver. He jogs up to her and when he reaches her, he nudges Sheila a bit and says, "it's okay. She doesn't need the ride."

"What did you do that for?" she frowns as the taxi sped along a road of busy cars. He smiles apologetically at her and says, "I'm sorry. Ryan was being an ass and made me stay back. That's why I couldn't join you for lunch."

Sheila rolls her eyes. It's windy and her fringes are bothering her. Her hair's tied into a top bun and her reading glasses slide down her nose a bit as she fidgets with her hair.

"It's alright, Adrian . . . but you just lost me my ride home!"

"I'm going to treat you. Come on, there's the awesome coffee shop around the corner.

Sheila raises her eyebrows at him. "Treat, eh?"

"Yeah . . . wait—no, no, no! I meant it like friends not a date —"

"Yeah, yeah," she waves her hand. "I get it. Let's go then."

•••

Für Elise.

The first time he had come here, it was with Carmen. That was about two weeks ago and ever since, they've been daily customers.

When he pushes open the door, bells chime and he smiles as the smell of coffee washes over him. There're orange rounded table with black chairs and it's almost empty today. Granted the peaceful atmosphere and awesome coffee and scones, Für Elise wasn't really popular.

And Adrian doesn't mind that at all. He liked to be in the quiet.

"Wow," he hears Sheila sigh. "This looks beautiful."

There's a black board with today's special hung on a window and there're vases of lilies placed on every table. Adrian smiles at her and says, "Told you so. Come on."

Adrian walks to the last table in a far off corner because he always preferred sitting there. Sheila sits across him and they sit in silence, letting the soft music do its job.

Sheila chuckles, "The music's Für Elise too! The owner must be a real Beethoven fan, eh?"

"Must be." He fishes out his phone from the pocket of his black jacket and types a quick message to Carmen.

ADRIAN: *I'll be home late.*

CARMEN: *ur ditching me for some hot chick?!?!?*

ADRIAN: *You're too dramatic. I'll be back pretty soon, though. Why don't you invite Akelard or something?*

CARMEN: *hes sick, dummy. ill invite Jeroën????*

"You know, I'm starting to think that I'm boring you." Sheila's amused voice echoes in Adrian's head. He looks up hastily and croaks, "oh no. I was just texting my friend to tell her that I'll be late."

"Can I take your order—Oh hey Adrian?"

Adrian grins as he sees Nora with her clipboard and white uniform. "Hey! I thought your shift started from six?"

"Oh, Miranda couldn't come today and I was free so, ta-da!" she says and looks over at Sheila.

"Uh, Sheila? This is—"

"Hello, Nora," smiles Sheila. "I'm Sheila"— she flicks her thumb at Adrian— "this guy's college mate."

"Hey. Adrian always comes with Carmen and sometimes with Akelard so . . . what would two like to order?"

"The usual."

"Uh . . ." says Sheila, biting her pink lip. "What's today's special?"

"Today's special? Err . . . well, there's this chocolate brownie which tastes *delicious* but it's also the unhealthiest thing on the menu so . . ."

"I'll have that," she grins widely and Adrian smiles at the sight of her smile, "and a raspberry smoothie."

"So this is your order: raspberry scones, black coffee, a chocolate brownie and a raspberry smoothie?"

They nod and Nora clicks her tongue in approval before skipping to the kitchen.

"So, you and Carmen, huh?"

"What? Oh no, we're just friends," he says. "I don't know why people always assume that we're dating."

"How did you guys meet?"

"A long time back," he says absentmindedly. "If you want, I can take you to our apartment and introduce you to her."

Sheila's eyes run all over his face and it's almost like she's assessing him until she grins and says, "Okay!"

• • •

Adrian sees a pair of black sport shoes on the 'WELCOME' mat. Sighing deeply, he whispers to Sheila, "Now look. There's a really weird guy in there and if his presence really bothers you, just say the word and I'll drop you to your house, alright?"

Before Sheila could voice her reply, the door opens slowly and Carmen pops her head out.

"Oh, it's you," she says flatly, opening the door wider.

"Who were you expecting?" Adrian snorts. "Queen Elizabeth?"

Carmen opens her mouth to retort but when she spots Sheila, she closes it immediately.

"Carmen, *this* is Sheila," he says, "Sheila, *this* is Carmen."

"Hello," they say concurrently and chuckle. "Hi," Carmen says with a smile. "Adrian's told me a lot about you."

"Has he?" smirks Sheila as Adrian's cheek tint red. "Well, I could say the same for you."

"Come in, then!"

The duo step in and Adrian has almost forgotten about Jeroën until he sees Jeroën perched on the counter, munching on fries.

His bony face and his joined eyebrows freak the living daylights out of Adrian but then again, there's that atmosphere around him.

"Sheila," whispers Jeroën and jumps off the counter. He walks stiffly towards her and bows.

Sheila lets out a nervous laugh and when Jeroën lifts his head up, they talk with their eyes. Carmen and Adrian's eyes drift back and forth.

"You two know each other?" Carmen asks curiously.

"Uh yeah. Jeroën and I—we go a long way back."

Adrian blinks and sighs, "yeah, whatever. Let's watch a movie or something."

• • •

"What the *hell* do you think you're doing?" Adrian hisses as Carmen sticks her tongue out in concentration.

"I'm trying to sneak a picture of him," she says and they look at Jeroën who's talking very discreetly to Sheila. Carmen's hiding behind the counter with her phone in her hand.

"And why would you do that?" asks Adrian. When he had seen Carmen disappear to the kitchen, he had taken the opportunity and excuse to leave the den only to find her here.

"Tomorrow's my appointment with Dr. Melissa." When Adrian shoots her a questioning look, she says, "The psychologist? I thought I'd just take a picture of him to show her in case she asked."

"Oh. What time is it?"

"It's at 12 in the afternoon. Hold on—"

Click.

"Got it!" she squeals excitedly. "I got it!"

"I feel like a stalker," he mutters.

"And *I* feel like I'm going mad."

•••

Chapter 7

Carmen Lets Out a Shaky Breath

Adrian is seated on a chair and he gives her a comforting smile. She returns it, just a bit nervously, wipes her sweaty hands on her shorts and pushes the door.

A strong smell of a mix of medicines and some scent that she can't really put her finger on, washer over her and it makes her cringe. She shuts the door and looks around.

Dr. Melissa's room looked more like an office. The walls had some kind of floral sticker on them and there was this huge bureau on which there were stacks of papers. Dr. Melissa, a plump woman in her early-fifties, smiles at her and gestures her to take a seat.

"Hello," smiles Carmen sitting on a wooden chair near to where Dr. Melissa sat.

"Hello, dear. Your name is Carmen—?"

"Carmen Collins."

"Right," hums the doctor, whisking through a few pages of her big file. She looks up and her green eyes twinkle with knowledge. "And what are you studying in college?"

"Architecture, ma'am. In Berkley?"

"Nice," she smiles, her frail lips revealing a set of white teeth. "My son's an architect too. But he studies in Massachusetts."

Carmen nods, pleased with the small conversation. Her nervousness is slowly ebbing away.

"So, Carmen," says the doctor, putting on her spectacles. "What exactly is the problem?"

"Um, okay. So, there's this guy . . . who I think, looks very handsome but the thing is, the people around me, they find him very ugly."

"Oh. When did you first meet him?"

"August 21st. At my uncle's wedding. Uh, if it's going to help you in anyway, I have his picture."

"You do?" The doctor grins. "Could you show me, please?"

Carmen fishes out her phone from her cardigan. She sees that Adrian sent her a message saying that he had to leave as Akelard had called him. Rolling her eyes, she goes to her photo gallery, clicks on Jeroën's picture and hands it over to the doctor.

Dr. Melissa's reaction's almost comical. At first, she screws up her eyebrows. Then, she frowns and pushes the phone away. "Is this the boy?"

"Uh, ye—"

"But, my dear, he is indeed very ugly."

"I know!" snaps Carmen. "But I don't see him like that!"

Dr. Melissa sighs drearily. "You know these are quite like the symptoms of madness?"

Carmen pales and her hands are shivering. "You're telling me that . . . ?"

"We could do a few tests and—"

"But I'm not mad!" she yells. "I'm NOT mad. This is just—"

"You're going through denial right—"

Carmen's fuming now. She stands up and her chair falls. Snatching her phone, she glares and says, "thank you."

And without waiting for a shout of protest, she speeds out of the room.

• • •

Cars are honking and the sound makes her go wild as tries to cross the busy road. It's raining and she's completely drenched and she hopes that her tears are disguised as raindrops. Her feet lands on puddles and water splashes onto her black leggings.

She heaves a sigh of relief as she reaches the sidewalk. People are staring at her but for once, it doesn't bother her. She wipes her wet red face which matched her red hair as she runs down the sidewalk.

"Hey! Watch where you're going!"

"God, what the hell?! Are you blind?"

"You made me drop my sandwich!"

The rain has stopped. She's crying but she can't stop. She doesn't know where she's going but she kept running. That was until she steps on someone's foot. She stops running veers around to apologise but when she turns around, she's face to face with a hooded person.

"Carmen?"

No, no, no, no. She doesn't want to see him now. She tries to go but Jeroën's firm grip on her arm is preventing her from doing so.

"Let me go!" she cries. She realises that now, there aren't much people around her. She's in a dark alley with a couple of teenage boys on one end of the corner, smoking.

"Are you crying? He demands. "Why are you crying?"

"It's none of your business!" She can see his grey eyes narrow. "Let me go, *please!*"

"What is wrong?" He asks and Carmen can *feel* his anger rolling off his body like waves.

"Um—" she says, letting out a shaky breath. "I just found out that my . . . um, dog? He died." She finished lamely, picking on a loose piece of yarn of her cardigan.

"What is wrong?" he asks again. "You are lying to me."

"No, I'm no—"

"You are lying—"

"Fine!" she snaps angrily. "You want to know what's wrong." And she takes a deep breath and starts to yell. "I'm mad! And it's all because of you! You're the reason for all this! First: I'm fearless which makes me abnormal! Second: You. I . . . who are you?!" He voice goes a higher octave. "Who the hell are you? What are you, some kind of magician who changes his appearance all the time? How is it that . . . I see you as handsome and the other see you as ugly? Is that normal?"

" . . ."

"It's not," she sniffs. "You know, I'm supposed to be used to this. This whole—abnormal deal? Everyone knows it!" She chuckles mirthlessly. "Adrian tells him that I give off this vibe—this . . . fearless vibe but really? I—"

"Wait." His voice is stoic and firm. There's a tint of coldness in it too and Carmen can feel a shiver crawling up her back. "How . . . you are fearless."

She's tempted to retort a snarky comment but instead, she nods.

"You *are* really fearless."

Jeroën lets go off her arm hastily. She can hear the boys laughing at something.

"She told me to like . . . stop but I didn't!"

"Whoa, bad ass, eh?"

"You bet your mom's Jimmy Choo's I am!"

"That is obvious," Jeroën mutters. "I do not know how it slipped my mind. You are"— his grey eyes shine and it makes her knees wobble —*"fearless."*

". . ."

"Well, we are going to your apartment," he says, catching Carmen's hand and pulls her out of the alley.

"Hey!" She protests. "What are you doing?"

Jeroën looks at her and his hood reveals a few strands of his black. "Oh, trust me, Carmen. You are anything but mad."

• • •

"Please, don't," Carmen begs as Jeroën pulls her towards the door. "If Adrian sees me like this, he's going to flip and if he sees you—"

Ding dong.

"Coming!" The door flings open and Adrian stares incredulously at Carmen. "What're you doing here?" He asks Carmen. "I thought that it would take two hours."

". . ."

"Have you been crying? And why are you drenched with water?" Adrian asks, looking concerned.

She doesn't answer as she takes a sudden interest in her white sport shoes. Adrian looks at Jeroën and his calm demeanour changes. He's shaking with rage and if Adrian's green eyes could change colours, they would be a screaming red.

"What the *fuck* is he doing here?" Carmen's eyes widen. Adrian never really said the F—word. He always found it vile and immature.

"Move," Jeroën orders. When Adrian doesn't budge a bit, Jeroën's hood falls off.

Adrian and Carmen gape as Jeroën's grey eyes turn darker and it seems as though Adrian's in a trance. His face is going pale, really pale.

"What—what—"

"Move."

This time Adrian moves and Jeroën blinks and when he does, the paleness ebbs away and it's replaced with Adrian's tanned face.

"What . . ." mutters Carmen as Jeroën enter the apartment like he owned it. Adrian looks at Carmen with fear and says, "I bet you a million dollars that he's not human."

• • •

Chapter 8

Adrian is a Broad Minded Person

Back when he was in school, grade seven (to be precise), Mary Cue, one of the popular girls had started talking about some werewolf story she had read. Normally, Adrian wouldn't give two hoots about what Mary spoke because all that came out of Mary's mouth was garbled rubbish. *That* was until she told them about how people would change into werewolves when they turned sixteen.

Adrian had believed that he was one. After all, he was hot, strong and muscular. Perfect alpha material.

And here he is. Eighteen and still waiting for that transformation.

"Cars?" He mutters as Jeroën paces around the room, his hands stuck deep in his jacket. He looks like he's having an internal battle with himself.

"What?" she whispers. Her red wet hair is plastered all over her face and she's shivering. She peels off her cardigan.

"He might be a werewolf."

Carmen looks at Adrian with an *'are-you-kidding-me-right-now?'* look. He smiles sheepishly and whispers fiercely, "I mean, his eyes darkened. And who knows? He might belong to another clan of werewolves in which they can change their appearance and—"

"Twilight really isn't applicable for all cases, Adrian."

His cheeks flame. "I've never read Twilight!"

The look Carmen gives him tells him that she's having none of it.

"Okay," Jeroën says. "Take a seat both of you."

Carmen gives Adrian a glare before he can open his mouth to retort. They sit on their bean bags obediently. Jeroën take a deep breath and look at the both of them.

Adrian cringes.

Carmen smiles softly.

"What I am going to tell you," he says robotically, "will seem very strange to you and you will not believe me"—Adrian snorts —"but Carmen, *you* are not mad."

"Are you finally admitting that there's something wrong with you? Adrian asks.

"Yes."

"See? I told you Carmen! *You* are not mad"— he flicks his thumb to Jeroën who raises an expectant eyebrow —"he—"

"—is a werewolf?" she finished flatly, folding her arms.

"A werewolf?" says Jeroën in distaste. They snap their heads at him and see him with an incredulous look on his face. "God Almighty! A werewolf, you call me?" And then, he throws his head back and starts to laugh.

Unlike his whole ug—horrible appearance, his laughter is rich. It's manly and . . . Adrian doesn't know if he can call a laugh strong.

Because it sounds pretty strong.

"Ha, *Iudex* is probably laughing up there!" He cackles and out of the blue, thunder roars. Adrian gives out a little feminine yelp while Carmen rolls her blue eyes.

"So much for manliness," she mutters and Adrian makes a childish face at her.

"Okay, can you stop laughing and just tell us what's wrong with you?"

Jeroën's eyebrows shoot up and he smirks. "*I am someone you would never imagine.*"

"Oh. Kay." Adrian narrows his eyebrows.

"I," says Jeroën with an air of finality, "am Death."

Silence.

Adrian who always had the record of breaking awkward silences, snorts and says, "Yeah, and I'm Obama's son. Give me a break."

Carmen sighs and says, "Look Jeroën. As much as we would—"

"You think that I am lying?" He says incredulously.

"Uh, yes, we do?"

"Shut up, Adrian."

"How do I make you two believe me?" He asks, cocking his head to the side.

"Simple!" Adrian grins a little two widely. Pointing at the door, he says, "You can start by leaving."

Jeroën narrows his eyes and says, "I know how to."

"Yeah, bucko. *Everyone* knows how to leave."

Jeroën starts to unzip his jacket slowly. Adrian's green eyes widen and he quickly cups Carmen's eyes. "What on earth do you think you're doing?"

"I'm trying—"

"To strip in front of my innocent best friend?" He asks, looking mortified. "You're trying to show her—"

"*I'm* trying," he sneers and rips off the sleeves of his jacket, "to show her *this*."

Adrian's hands that are covering Carmen's eyes fall limply and plop on the bean bag. Carmen blinks a multiple number of times. When her green eyes land on Jeroën's arms, she freezes.

"Do you believe me, now?" Jeroën asks softly, his eyes landing on Carmen's shocked face.

His arms are covered with names that appear and vanish in seconds. It was like how ice dissolved in boiling water. Names appeared and disappeared and it almost seemed like tattoos.

Just, it wasn't exactly *tattooed*.

"What . . . what . . ." Adrian doesn't know what to ask. He doesn't know if he should ask *what* or *why* or *how*.

"That," Jeroën says, folding his arms, "is death. That is how many people die in time."

"That—I—"

"I would love to explain but the real question: would you two let me?"

They nod without a single word escaping their lips.

"I do not know how the people of this century refer to Death as. I do not know but I think the most popular one is The Grim Reaper, no?"

They do not respond.

Jeroën sighs wearily. "Anyways, I promise you that I do not carry a scythe that drags people's souls away and nor do I wear a cloak that makes me invisible."

"So . . ." Carmen says with her eyes still wide. "You're Death?"

"One of them, yes."

"What do you mean by that?"

"You know that saying? 'God could not be everywhere so he made mothers'?" Jeroën rolls his eyes. "Well, God could not exactly make *one* death to take away people's souls. So, he made many."

"So," Adrian gulps, his hands shivering, "there're more of you?"

"An infinite number, Adrian." Adrian feels shivers crawling down his spine and it's *not* in a sexual way.

"So, basically—"

"Let me explain, please. There're many Deaths, yes. But few of us come down here. You see, we reside or *live*," he snickers, "in Purgatory."

"I'm not a Catholic," claims Adrian. "I'm a universalist."

"Well then, we reside where all souls are cleansed. When humans die, they undergo through what is called the particular or individual judgement. You are judged instantly and you receive your award, for good or ill."

"Like, basically, we are cleansed from our sins?"

"Yes. *This* is done by the Authority. The Authority consists of two messengers: *Percontator* and *Iudex*."

"Say what?" Adrian asks dumbly.

"Per—con—ta—tor. Ee—you—they," says Jeroën clenching his jaw. "You are very slow."

"Carry on," Carmen says quickly when Adrian's face turns red.

"Yes. Yes. So, Percontator—which is the Latin word for 'The Interrogator'— basically, he is the one who interrogates the soul on their wrong and their rights. Iudex—which is the Latin word for 'The Judge'—basically, he is the one who cleanses each soul from their sins."

"This is crazy," mutters Adrian, running his hand through his brown curls.

"Um, so, who's the most powerful?" asks Carmen looking unfazed by all the information.

"Iudex, of course."

"Err, why are you here if you reside in Purgatory?" Adrian asks, trying to look at anywhere but Jeroën's arms.

"As I have told you before, there are an infinite number of deaths and all of us are assigned to different places *but* there are exceptions." Jeroën pauses and Carmen strongly suspects that it is for a dramatic effect. "Since, you know, Death is a very delicate occurrence and . . . being—"

"How so?" asks Adrian.

"Our deeds revolve around grief and pain and everything negative. It is easy for us to lose interest in what we are doing because, as I said before, we are exposed to feeling and since we are delicate, there are times when we succumb to such feelings."

"Like . . . love?" asks Carmen.

Jeroën's steely gaze softens as it lands on her. "I prefer sympathy. When we lose interest, we start questioning what we're doing and why we are doing it and when we *question*, we become more . . . human. The Authority, to prevent this, sends those who are in the doubtful stage to Earth so that we can be like normal human beings and observe the world."

"How does that help?"

"We're exposed to all the bad in this world. We learn about the colder side of the world," he says, his grey eyes piercing through Carmen, "and when we're fully devoid of all feelings, we return to Purgatory or . . . whatever you would like to call the place where you cleanse your sins."

Adrian and Carmen try to process the information. It seems fitting and yet, it doesn't. "What do I have to do with this?" Carmen asks softly.

"Nothing much," informs Jeroën. "You are bothered with my appearance." He strolls over to Carmen and bends a little. "What do you think of Death, Carmen?"

Death?

Carmen had learned to accept death a long time ago with the death of her father and brother. Her mother had died giving birth to her brother. She had been exposed to the doings of Death from a young age.

"Um . . . I—I don't know. I just . . . think it's a natural occurrence. Something that's bound to happen to everyone."

"And you, Adrian?" He shifts his eyes to Adrian. Adrian clenches his jaw and looks away because he knows that if he looks into his eyes, he'll spill everything out.

"Exactly," Jeroën whispers. "You accept reality. Others do not. Whoever is scared of death will see me as ugly. Whoever accepts death —reality, will see me as handsome." He smiles, "You are fearless."

"So . . ." she croaks, her hands sweating. "Everyone else is . . . scared of you?"

"Most of them, yes. Death after all, depends on perception. Just like religion and . . . love."

"So, is this supposed to help her feel better?" scowls Adrian. "That we're face to face with someone who brings destruction?"

"Death," sneers Jeroën, his eyes a darker shade, "is never related to *destruction*. Destruction is something you're not even aware of."

"*Wait*. Back at the door, you did something to me. What—"

"Parts of your soul were leaving you, yes." Jeroën nods.

"So, I almost died?!" Adrian asks mortified.

"Aha, you have a long way from death, Adrian. That, I can assure you."

Adrian scowls at him. He doesn't want to accept this as easily as Carmen is. "This doesn't solve—"

"You are good friends with Sheila, are you not?"

"What's this got to do with her?" He asks defensively.

Jeroën chuckles. "The fact that you're oblivious to what she is, is highly amusing. Adrian," he smirks, "*she* is one the daughters of Iudex."

Adrian freezes and he can slowly feel his hands going limp. "Iu . . . no . . . how . . ."

"Sheila is someone who belongs to the upper world. She is not human. No one really understood her request to live in Earth but Iudex allowed her. He believed that like Death, she would be tired of humans and come back."

"But?"

"But she didn't. Unlike us, she found more light in the world. I do not know by what she meant, but she did. She found that there was equal happiness and good. Iudex and she are in some sort of conflict at the moment."

Carmen sighs. "Are we the only humans who know this?"

"No. It is expected for the Deaths who are sent down to earth to mingle with humans. Very few are accepted by society and very few humans know of this. Count yourselves lucky."

Sheila's hazel brown eyes have a mysterious glint in them when she says, "don't bother. I come from a place far out of your reach."

"Far out of my reach," he mutters. Dropping his head into his hands, he murmurs, "Oh God."

"I will let you two digest the information. It is hard for any human to take in anything like this. Have a nice night."

• • •

Chapter 9

Carmen is Exceptionally Talented at Avoiding People

She had started avoiding people from a young age. She hated looking at people who looked at her in distaste. Her brother was a social butterfly and her father often used to tell her to be like him. She couldn't, though. Back then, she was rebuked because she was fearless. No one talked to her. However, Ben was always in the spotlight. He looked good and scored well in academics and sports.

He was the Golden Boy.

She remembers the day when she got the call. She remembers Uncle Joe coming to her with tears streaming down his face.

"They're gone, Cars. They're gone."

She remembers nodding mutely and she remembers kissing her father and brother's pale faces. She remembers the pitiful looks her family members cast her. She remembers the advice they gave her.

"At least try and be normal, now."

She remembers the guilt, the anger, the pain. Oh, she remembers it all.

"You okay, Carmen?"

Carmen looks at Layla. Her caramel skin looks lighter than usual as the sunlight glistens on her face. "Yeah, I'm fine," she smiles tightly. "Where's Omar? I didn't see him in my Physics class."

Layla rolls her eyes. "He's sick. It was raining yesterday and he went out to 'feel the rain'. Well, he certainly did which is why he's stuck at home."

"That sounds like something Adrian would do," Carmen grins. Layla winks at her and pulls her closer making a few drops of Carmen's coffee land on her floral dress. Layla didn't seem to mind, though. "Can I just ask why that creep is staring at you?"

"Jeroën?" she gulps.

Layla nods, sneaking a glance at him. She shivers and says, "I really don't want to be rude but he's just too . . ."

"Ugly?"

"Yes," sighs Layla. "But I have to give you something for befriending him. That's really nice of you. Just a question though," she says, biting her lip, "how do you . . . how can you talk to him without cringing in disgust?"

Carmen laughs nervously. "Ha—ha. I mean . . . uh, I feel like it's really rude and he feels really bad so—"

Someone clears their throat.

Carmen cringes discreetly but doesn't look up. She can see Layla gulp. She takes out her notebook and pretends to read through all the notes she had written without Omar's help.

"Hey, Jeroën!" smiles Layla. Carmen can see how strained the smile and she has this urge to laugh.

"Hello," he says remotely. "Can I borrow your friend for a few minutes?"

Carmen notices that the ground is quiet. No one's giggling or gossiping or eating. They're just staring at Jeroën in fear and disgust. Not wanting Layla to be shunned away, she stands up and smiles tightly. "Let's go Jeroën."

He clutches her hand and she can *feel* some kind of rippling shock go through her hand and she winces slightly. Jeroën sees this and he smirks slightly. Carmen tries to ignore how good he looked when he smirks.

He pulls her out of the grounds and into an empty corridor. A few professor nod politely at Carmen and try to do the same to Jeroën but they just can't. They look away immediately.

Jeroën looks into through the glass that is on the door of every lecture theatre. Seeing nobody, he opens the door and pulls Carmen in. As soon as he shuts the door, Carmen wrenches her hand from his strong grip.

"What're we doing here?"

"Talking," he says and scowls. "Are you trying to avoid me, Carmen?"

Carmen lets out a sarcastic laugh. "Pfft. Oh me? Definitely not. I'm definitely not trying to ignore Death himself."

"Jeroën. The name is Jeroën and it is quite smart if you do not avoid me. You possess important information. You do not really think that I'll let you go, do you?"

It would've sounded romantic had it not been Death.

"Fine," she sighs reluctantly, "I was avoiding you. I mean, learning all about you . . . sure, it assured me that I'm not mad but . . ." she falters, "I'm still fearless and—"

"You know," says Jeroën with a smile. "Being fearless can be both a bane and a boon at the same time. I understand how you feel. It is true; you cannot experience all the thrilling things in life but guess what? You are more exposed to reality. You do not cower in fear and to be honest, that is really impressive."

Carmen blushes and says, "Thanks but I just . . . can't see you as how I used to see you."

"Why?" He asks worriedly. "Do I not look handsome? What changed? Is it the hair? I tried to do a new hairstyle—you know, with my hair standing and—"

"A Mohawk?" Carmen chuckles. She looks at his black hair and raises and eyebrow. "It looks the same."

He frowns. "I was trying to go for a new look. What a bother, though. I wasted . . . like half an hour on it."

Carmen raises her arm daintily and touches his hair as though his hair is some kind of rare artefact. His black hair is messed up as usual and it feels *really soft*. She keeps rummaging through his hair and his eyes close slowly.

As though he's relishing the moment.

Her eyes widen and she retracts her hand hastily. He snaps his grey eyes open and he looks at her with a questioning look. She blushes profusely and stammers, "Uh—Um, I have to go. I have Geometry next!"

She rushes out.

• • •

"Hello?"

There's some murmuring in the background and Carmen furrows her eyebrows as nobody responds. "Hello?" she asks again.

"He—hello?"

"Joe!" she squeal, her face flooding with excitement. "God, it's actually you!"

"Yeah. I'm honoured that you think I'm God—"

"Seriously?"

Uncle Joe laughs and Carmen remembers how life was like living with him. "I missed you too, Cars. So, tell me, how're things with you?"

"Great, great," she says, pacing around her room. "How's Lucia?"

"Oh she's—hey! Let me talk to her! Yeah, whatever," he grumbles. "She's fine."

"Having your first fight already, eh?" she asks teasingly.

"Oh *sure*," he drawls. "How's Adrian? What about college? Did you make any friends?"

"Whoa, one at a time, please," she chuckles, "Adrian's great. He's in college, right now. I'm home because it's a half day today. College is great, Uncle Joe. It's so huge and—"

"Carmen?" asks Uncle Joe, softly. "What about friends?"

"Don't worry, Joe. There's Omar and Layla and . . . Jeroën . . ."

"Oh. Oh. Jeroën Jarvis?"

". . . Yeah," she says slowly. "Do you know him?"

"I knew his dad, yes. He used to work with me. Poor old chap died, though."

"How?"

"He fell down the stairs." Joe pauses. "Don't be too hard on Jeroën, Cars. I mean, I get it that he looks shitty but—"

"We're pretty good friends, Joe," she smiles. *Death has a father?*

"Oh," he sighs in relief. "Well, we'll be back in two weeks. *We* have a lot to see."

"Right. Bye."

Carmen sets her phone down and starts to do her homework.

• • •

"I don't understand this!" he fumes, clutching his curls.

"It's s—simple," Akelard gulps at Adrian's foul mood. "Uh—should I say I—it again?"

"No!" he scowls. The librarian and a couple of students glare at him. He makes sure to glare back at them with equal ferocity.

"What crawled up his back and died?"

Adrian closes his eyes in frustration. The last voice he wants to hear right now is *hers*. Her amused voice just sets him off.

"U—um, he didn't u—understand some t—topic in Civil P-Procedure."

"Any idiot can understand Civil Procedure," she muses and sits on the seat across Adrian. He looks up and scowls. "Well, *sorry*. I'm not so smart, then!"

"What's with the attitude?" she frowns. "You're not acting like you do as usual." She looks at Akelard who gives her a nervous smile and an unsure shrug. Sheila leans closer and says, "Is something wrong, Adrian?"

His sturdy gaze softens at her concern.

"Oh, it's nothing, really. I just found out that my friend and I know Death—a death and just found out that this girl who has really caught my attention is actually the daughter of some judge guy high up in Purgatory."

"I'm fine," he sighs wearily. "Sorry. I'm just in a foul mood."

"I figured," she chuckles. Grabbing his book, she cocks an eyebrow. "Do ou want me to explain this to you?"

He nods. "Hey, Akelard. You can join too. You had some difficulty with this topic, right?"

"Y—yes."

As she explains, Adrian's not listening. He stares at how elegant her face looks. She did have an air of serenity and purity. Almost like an angel. Her voice was soft and kind and even Akelard started to warm up to her.

That night, Adrian slept without facing any nightmares.

• • •

Chapter 10

Adrian is in Shock

Because it's not every day when you find out that the girl who had fervently tried to flirt with you commits suicide.

Candice Ferguson.

"I don't know, man," whispers Ryan. "It's like, she sends me a text to meet her in her dorm and when I come, lo, she's hanging from the ceiling.

Adrian doesn't answer. He nods mutely, rubbing his sweaty forehead. She's gone. Gone.

"It's so sad!" blubbers Stacy. "We always used to—"

"Stop," Adrian says hoarsely. "Stop trying to recollect memories. Just . . . stop."

He taps his fingers on his Civil Law book. That feeling of surprise and . . . something (that he can't put his finger on) washes over him. It's strange because the seat that she used to sit on (right across him) looks like its mocking his inability to understand what she went through. He always used to think that she was one who was all brawn and no brain. She was one who always looked at him with a sultry look in her eyes.

"Do they know why . . . ?"

"They say that she wrote a six-page suicide note that was found by her dad. There was something about an abortion or something," shrugs Fatima, popping her bubble gum.

"That sucks, man."

"Totally, dude."

And then, guilt hits him. He had blatantly ignored her advances last week because he really despised desperate girls. What if she had wanted to talk to him?

"Hey," he whispers hoarsely to Akelard. Akelard might as well be invisible because no one really noticed him. "How 'bout we skip the rest of college?"

• • •

"Um, a—are y—you okay?"

"I'm fine, Akelard," Adrian sighs. He pours in his milk and watches how the milk swirls in the back coffee.

And it strangely fascinated him.

"You okay, though?" He asks looking at Akelard who's sitting on their breakfast table. "You look really droopy."

"I—I'm f—fine." He smiles weakly.

"Why don't you take a nap, then?"

He doesn't object. He nods unquestioningly and gets up, his eyelids half closed.

"Hey, where're you going?" Adrian asks looking confused as Akelard strolls over to the door.

"T—to my a—apartment," he stammers.

"Didn't you tell me this morning that your broke the cot by dropping your bookshelf on it?" he deadpans.

"R-right. I—I forgot," he blushes. Adrian rolls his eyes and says, "You can take a nap in my room. I'll watch some TV."

After Akelard retires to bed, Adrian walks over to his kitchen and puts on his apron. He's officially the chef of the apartment. He takes out a pan from the shelf and sets it on the stove.

Why had she committed suicide? He tries to recollect if he ever saw a fleeting look of dismay or sadness on her face.

Never.

So maybe, he isn't the only one wearing a mask. Maybe he's not the only one fakes a smile and tries to act all manly.

The world is indeed a paradox.

• • •

"I'm home!" she yells, kicking off her tennis shoes and throws her bag on the sofa. She raises an eyebrow at the quietness and mentally slaps herself. *Of course*, Adrian wouldn't be there. He'd be at college now.

Then, she bites her lip in confusion. She did see a pair of black Nikes on the threshold which definitely belonged to Adrian. Her ears perk up at the sound of gushing water that came from the guest toilet.

She rolls her eyes and plods over to the toilet. She grips the handle and without bothering to knock, she pushes it open.

Akelard's face is stricken with tears and he's in his pale white airy boxers holding up a pair of drenched pants. He's shivering and chokes on his sob as he turns around quickly and stares at Carmen's pale blue eyes.

"I—I d—" He starts to cry. His face is red with shame and pain. Carmen mutely nods before leaving. She walks over to Adrian's room and sees the sheets ruffled. The covers are pulled out. She sighs and pulls out a pair of pyjama pants from Adrian's cupboard and picks up the wet covers.

"Hey," she says softly, pushing the door a little so that she could slip in the pyjamas. "You can use these and sleep in tonight and don't bother washing them. I do have to do the laundry today, anyways."

He grabs the pyjama pants and smothers his face into it before crying loudly. She hears a loud sleepy groan from her room which she guesses to be Adrian.

"I—The covers and—"

"I get it," she whispers. "Come on. Why don't you just wash your face and leave your pants there and put on those pyjamas. I heard about your cot. You can sleep in Adrian's room."

"No—No! I'll sleep on the couch, please."

"Okay. Whatever makes you comfortable."

When he doesn't move, she gently pulls him out and gives him a kind smile.

"It's okay."

He nods shakily before scurrying off into Adrian's room. After putting the covers and Akelard's pants in the laundry, she stretches and lets out a deep yawn.

She whistles some familiar tune as she walks over to her room. Adrian's half awake as he watches her pull the covers over herself with half lidded eyes.

"What was all that?" His voice is laden with sleep. "Who was crying?"

"It doesn't matter," she says. "Go to sleep."

He groans and rubs the crust from his eyes. "A girl from my college committed suicide yesterday."

She lies on her back and throws back her arms, resting them under head. Frowning, she looks at Adrian and says, "Really? How come I didn't hear of that?"

"I don't know," he sighs. "I just feel terrible."

"Were you two like . . . close or something?"

"No. No, she was just . . . I mean, she always used to flirt with me and if I remember correctly, last week she really did try to talk to me and I just brushed her off because . . . you know how much I despise desperate girls"— he runs his hands through his curls and lets out a frustrated sigh — "how was I—what if she really wanted to talk to me?"

Carmen doesn't say anything.

"It's funny how I keep forgetting that I'm not the only one trying so hard to put a smile on my face. It seems that she had written a letter and there was something about an abortion . . . It sucks, really. It does and it makes me wonder"— he looks at Carmen — "how many of the people I know are actually smiling out of happiness?"

"Look, Adrian," she says softly. "Everyone has their masks and I keep telling you that. Some of us put it on a little early, some of us put it on a little late and if we keep moaning about how it hurts and shit, nothing's going to work out. The thing is, we're all interrupted with *our* problems and we don't really bother to observe the people around us." She smiles and ruffles Adrian's hair. "That's what's you're going through. Let's just say that she's in a happier place now."

"Huh, yeah," he sighs. "Anyways, did you eat the pasta I made you?"

"Um, no."

"It's in the fridge. Do you want—"

She lets out a fake yawn. "Nope. Nada. I'm *really* sleepy right now."

Adrian narrows his eyes at her. "I promise that this pasta's much better."

"Go to sleep, Adrian. I really don't want to be affected my food poisoning right now."

"You suck."

"You swallow. By the way—" she says quickly before Adrian can mouth his reply. "I just found out your Skype password."

Adrian blushes a dark red. "Yeah right," he snorts, coughing.

She gives him a flat look. "Yeah, 'Adrian rocks underscore you don't'," she recites with a smirk. *"Really?"*

"I hate you," he grumbles. "I was just being original. You should go to sleep, now."

"Sure," she drawls with an amused smile. "Have a nice nap, 'Adrian rocks underscore you don't'."

"You too—hey wait!"

• • •

Chapter 11

Carmen Bites Her Lip in Frustration

She should've *known* that this day would come. The day their roles would reverse.

Today, she's the cook.

"What are you standing there like a statue?" groans Adrian. He pushes the bowl of murky green soup and says, "Try and make something more edible next time!"

"But I don't know how to cook, Adrian!" she whines.

"I've told you how to"— he coughs — "do it many times. Just . . . don't add too much salt."

His forehead is sweaty and he's having difficulty in breathing. He reaches out to his bedside table and pulls out a tissue from his tissue box.

"How 'bout I just make you some hot chocolate?" she offers. As far as she was aware, hot chocolate was the only thing that she knew how to make without making anyone puke it out.

"I've drunk two cups already," he glares. "You'd be a horrible housewife."

Carmen bites her lip uneasily. She did feel a bit guilty for not taking care of him like he had taken care of her whenever she was sick.

"Call Akelard, would you?" He groans. "Hopefully, he'll be better than you."

"Um, I did try calling him but his phone's switched off and he's not opening the door."

"Hey," he says slowly. "You didn't tell 'bout—"

The doorbell rings.

Please be Akelard, she prays. She stumbles on her boots that are in the hallway and kicks it away in frustration.

Ding dong.

"Coming!" she yells. "God!" She groans. The chairs of the dining table are strewn in the hallway and Carmen silently curses Adrian for acting like a drunkard when he's sick.

Ding dong ding dong ding dong.

She can hear Adrian give out a loud groan at the continuous ringing of the bell. It almost seemed like a tune to her.

She flings the door open and gawks.

"Good afternoon," says Jeroën with a charming grin. "May I come in?

"Y—why are you here?" she squeaks. He has his hood pulled up and she can see a few black strands peeking out.

"CARMEN!" yells Adrian.

"What?" she snaps. "I'm coming, you ass!" Sighing, she pinches the bridge of her nose and opens the door wider. "Come in."

"Wait here." With that said, she leaves Jeroën in the den as she walks over to Adrian's room. He's leaning over the headboard with his six pack abs in full view. Most girls would drool and lick his feet being in such a situation but Carmen scrunches her nose. Adrian smirks and pulls the covers up to his chest before letting out a girlish shriek.

"Oh. Em. Gee! You saw my chest!" he squeals.

"My poor eyes," she mutters. "I'm going to make you some soup."

"Make sure it's edible and—"

She shuts the door.

• • •

"It says *one* table spoon—God, Jeroën! Do you have to do everything the straight opposite?"

"It is supposed to be two. It will taste better," he says. He sniffs the boiling soup and gives her thumbs up. She raises her eyebrows dubiously and scoffs.

"Please. You're Death. You wouldn't know what tastes good and what doesn't!"

"I may not be human but I do know a few things," he smirks. "And please, stop calling me Death. I prefer Jeroën."

"Sorry," she says biting her lower lip.

He doesn't reply. Instead, he pours out some healthy looking cream coloured liquid into a bowl. He claps his hands with a triumphant smile that melts Carmen's heart.

As she places the bowl of boiling soup on the tray, the smell of corn wafts by her nostrils and she lets out a pleasant sigh. Not wanting to boost Jeroën's already boosted ego, she leaves the kitchen and walks to Adrian's room gingerly with Jeroën hot on her tail.

"*Monsieur?*" she says with a fake bow pushing the door a little. Adrian looks up from a magazine and a grin lights up his face. "*Puis-je entrer?*" She asks with her voice deeper.

"*Oui,*" he says in a posh accent. "*J'ai attendu pendant des siècles, milady.*"

Carmen straightens her back and smirks. *"Maître, ce que vous allez déguster maintenant est une delicasy rare—"*

"Get in," he groans and sniffs loudly. "I'm hungry!"

She lets out a chuckle before waltzing into the room. His eyes narrow in annoyance as she performs hideous dance steps taking one step at a time to reach his bed.

"I swear to everything I own, Cars—"

"Here!" she laughs giving him the bowl. "Blow on it. It's hot."

He gives her a flat look. "No kidding," he mutters before blowing onto spoon laden with soup. He drinks from it and his eyes close, as though relishing the taste.

He mumbles something incoherently. "What?"

"I said that this taste delicious," he moans, taking another sip. "You didn't make this," he says, his mouth full of corn soup. "Akelard did, didn't he?"

"*I* did, actually."

Adrian clenches his jaw as he takes in the figure leaning on the hinges of the door. "What're you doing here?"

"Adrian," says Carmen slowly. "Stop acting like a brat."

"Yes," drawls Jeroën with an unattractive smirk that makes Adrian recoil in disgust. "A 'thank you' would be nice."

Adrian snorts and pushes away the bowl of soup half heartedly. "I don't want this."

"Adrian, for Pete's sake! Stop acting like a jerk!" snaps Carmen, folding her arms. "I mean, I get—"

"It is not that I cannot make you eat it," Jeroën says, his voice husky, "but like Carmen, I get that you're not comfortable to me." His grey eyes glint dangerously and his lips curl into a cruel smirk.

Jeroën leaves and Adrian folds his arms, sulking. "Why did you—"

"Get some sleep," she sighs. "You're not acting like yourself."

• • •

"Um, I'm sorry about him," she says smiling apologetically. "Adrian can be a bit snappy . . . especially when he's sick."

"It is quite alright," he hums, taking a sip from his coffee. "Though, I assure you that it will be the same even when he is not sick."

"Yeah," she sighs, "he's not really used to the idea, yet."

"Like I said, it is alright. Forget Adrian. Tell me about yourself, Carmen."

Her porcelain skin turns red. "M—me? There's nothing much about *me*."

"Oh no. Certainly not. There must be *something*. Tell me, as someone who doesn't harbour any kind of feelings, I am curious to know which feeling you have not felt."

"Fear," she responds immediately.

He chuckles loudly and throws his legs over the arms of the couch. "Is there anything other than that?"

"Uh . . ." she says shyly, "that would be . . . love, I guess."

His thick black eyebrows rise up. "Love? You are telling me that you haven't felt love?"

"Not that kind of love. I mean there are two kinds of it, at least that's what I think."

". . . Right," he says slowly, looking genuinely intrigued.

"One is of course, the love you have for your family. That's quite natural. To love your family comes by instinct unless your family's really shitty or something and the other . . . is different. You now, that kind of feeling that you want to spend your life with one certain person because you believe that he or she will love you for who you are despite your flaws—"

"Hold on," says Jeroën holding up his hand. "Forgive me for interrupting you but what's the point having someone love you for who you are *despite* your flaws?"

Carmen shrugs. "Most people tend to hide their flaws so that no one uses it against them. It's quite rare to find someone who promises to never take advantage of your flaws."

"But . . . do your flaws not define who you are?"

Carmen gulps at the patronising look he's giving her. "M— Maybe . . . ?"

"I mean, at the end, possessions will crumble, beauty will fade but . . . your flaws still stay with you, right? After all, they *are* a part of your inner beauty."

"That . . . is an optimistic way of looking at things . . ."

"I thought that the thrill of life was all about seeing the light in everything and being aware of all the dark and vile things of life."

"Thrill?" she chuckles sarcastically. "I don't even know what thrill feels like."

"Neither do I," he responds quickly. "But one can hope, right? Can you not hope to feel thrill or love?"

"I try very hard to avoid hoping, to be honest."

"And why is that?"

"I detest hope. Hope is like . . . hanging on this delicate thread. It's weak and yet, it's strangely comforting but I try to never hope."

"Hm."

"Yeah. Hope is just . . . a temporary satisfaction. Like drugs. After some time, it's gone and you feel even horrible."

He stares at her for a few minutes and a crooked smile appears on his tanned face. "You're a pessimist, eh?"

"Nah. I'm just a realist," she smirks.

• • •

Chapter 12

Adrian Pretends to be Asleep

Akelard moans, "Get up, Adrian! I know you're not sleeping! You dropped Carmen to college half an hour ago. You're not fooling me by that snoring."

"..."

"I don't want to skip today!"

"Then don't." Adrian's voice comes out muffled due to the thickness of the covers.

"I knew you weren't sleeping!" he says triumphantly, his black eyes glinting with amusement.

So, Adrian's curly mop of brown curls emerges from the heaps of covers. "Your stuttering has improved."

"W—well, y—you know," he blushes, "it—it's—"

"Are you serious right now?"

"S—sorry. The—"

Adrian pulls the covers off and pats a spot next to him and says, "Sit down. Let's talk."

Akelard shyly sits on the edge of the bed and mutters, "A—about what?"

"About yourself. I know nothing about you."

"Th—There's not much to know . . ." he says softly, "it's nothing you wouldn't ha—have guessed, anyways."

Adrian furrows his eyebrows. "What do you mean?"

Akelard snickers coldly. "I bet Carmen has already told you a—about it and—"

"Whoa"— Adrian holds his hand up— "Carmen didn't tell me anything. What's going on?"

"Wait. Y—you're t—telling me that Carmen didn't tell you what happened day before y—yesterday?"

"No, she didn't. Wait"—he sits up so that his back's against the headboard— "Were you the one who cried?"

He blushes.

"What for? Why did you cry?"

"S—She . . . uh, found out a—about my . . ."

"Found out about what?" prompts Adrian.

"About my anxiety," he mumbles.

Adrian cocks his eyebrow as Akelard's hand starts to shiver. He clutches his cold fingers and asks softly, "How?"

"I—I . . . please don't stop being friends with me!" He rushes out, his black eyes widening in fear.

"Hey, hey. I won't."

"I—I peed when I was sleeping. I—I'm suffering from anxiety and . . . sometimes . . ."

". . . Okay . . ." Adrian says slowly. "I get it."

"I don't s—seem too w—weird, do I?"

"You don't," he chuckles. "Tell me about your family."

Akelard's face pales and his body starts to shiver uncontrollably. Adrian widens his eyes and says, "Hey, if you don't want to, it's okay. I promise it's fine and—"

"N—No, I want to tell you."

"Okay . . ."

"My p—parents k—kicked me out when I was fourteen. Th—They sent me to my aunt because I—I—"

"You don't really have to," says Adrian giving his hand a comforting squeeze.

Akelard shakes his head and whispers hoarsely, "No . . . I really want to. I—They kicked me out because I'm messed up."

"You're not messed up. Who said so?"

"Everyone in Berlin." When Adrian eyebrows rise up again, he explains, "I'm German. I don't have an accent because I was homeschooled by an American from a very young age. My parents—they kicked me out b—because I wasn't fit to be a part of Montouri family."

"Montouri?" Adrian feels a sense of familiarity strike him. "Wait . . . you don't happen to come from *the* Montouri family, do you? One of the biggest steel companies in Germany?"

He nods. "Yes. I—I have OCD and anxiety and my dad s—said that I—I would be a disgrace—no, I *am* a disgrace and then when I found out that I was gay, he was livid and he sent me to my aunt who lived in Texas and she was a really nice lady and she really took care of me, like,

I *really really* liked her but then, after two years, she passed away and I was shipped to my other aunt who really hated me and—"

"Whoa, whoa," snickers Adrian. "You're rambling. Calm down, bud."

Akelard blushes a dark red. "O—Of course. So, b—basically, I really hated it there so, I ran away from home."

"Really?" Adrian gasps, leaning forward. "You actually *ran* away from home?"

"Well, not *actually*. Like, I did run away but I got tired so I came back home."

"Real brave, bro."

"Sh—Shut up. A—Anyways, it sucked there but yeah. I haven't got in contact with my family ever since I came here and they haven't tried to contact me—obviously—so, it's n—not a big deal but . . ." Akelard sighs and closes his eyes.

"But?"

"According to the news, my mom gave birth to a baby girl five months ago. I"— he bites his lip and Adrian can see him clenching is jaw to hold back the tears— "don't even know her *name*. I don't know how she looks like."

Before Adrian could give him a hug, Akelard shakes his head and brushes away the unshed tears and looks up with a watery smile. He sniffs and says, "I just hope that they don't change her. What about you?"

Adrian bites his lip. He expected this and it almost makes him regret ever asking Akelard to tell him about his family. But when he looks into Akelard's black eyes, he sees sincerity and he feels a strange feeling of trust wash over him.

"Me? Uh, um. Well, my dad's a journalist and my mom . . . she, uh, she was a teacher at a special school."

Akelard smiles. "Sounds like a happy family."

Adrian chuckles darkly, his throat feeling dry. "Not really. My mom died when I was seven."

"Oh."

"Yup."

"Can I ask how?" Akelard asks meekly.

"Raped," Adrian muttered. "Um, she was coming back from school and she picked me up. We came home, she set the table and when we were eating dinner, *they* came."

"Y—You don' have t—to—"

"No, I want to. I want someone other than Carmen and my dad to know. Anyways, a couple of rogues came and they"—Adrian gulps—"raped her and made me w—w—"

Akelard sharply exhales, clutching the edge of the bed. "They made me watch it," he chokes out. "I—I couldn't really do anything. I . . . They took our money and left. When my dad came and found her, we rushed to the hospital but . . . she was long gone."

"Okay . . ." Akelard softly muttered. "Okay. F—Fine. That's enough for today."

"That's all there is, really."

". . ."

"Okay. So, I get a lot of nightmares of it."

"Every day?"

"Yup. Unless I sleep with Carmen. If I do, I don't really get them."

Akelard's face morphs from understanding to mortification. "Y— You don't h—have to tell me about your sex l—life!"

"I don't have sex with her!" he groans. "I just . . . sleep with her. Carmen's like my sister!"

"Oh."

"Yeah, *oh*."

• • •

"Huh, so you're gay?"

"Nope. I prefer Akelard."

"Shut up, smartass."

• • •

Carmen's giggling as she unlocks the door and steps inside with Jeroën. She throws off her boots and takes off her socks. She hears a lot of mumblings and chuckles coming from Adrian's room.

"Hey, why don't you sit down and switch on the TV and watch something?"

He shrugs and proceeds to do the same.

Carmen braces herself and tiptoes to Adrian's room and sees it a bit ajar. She pushes it a bit to see Adrian and Akelard seated against the headboard, chuckling at something on Adrian's laptop.

They look up, their body stiff with caution. When they see her standing by the door, they visibly relax. Adrian gives her a crooked grin and says, "We skipped college today."

"I can see that. What're you two doing?"

"Watching a movie."

"Well, just to give you two a heads-up, Omar and Layla are coming—"

"Who?" Akelard asks before blushing.

"My friends from college. Don't worry." She smiles comfortingly. "They're really nice."

"Okay," Adrian sighs. "Is Jeroën coming?"

"Nada," she says. "He doesn't want to."

"Good riddance."

"Adrian!"

• • •

"Hey!" Layla chirps holding up a packet. "We come bearing food."

"Welcome to our humble abode," Carmen bows as Adrian grins.

The couple shuffles in. "Yeah, so this is Adrian."

"Hey," Omar smiles, his blue eyes crinkling up. "We've heard a lot about you."

"All good things I hope?" Adrian chuckles, taking the plastic bag from Layla. "Oh! Tacos, eh?"

"Yup. Your apartment looks so lovely." Layla looks around their den that was particularly clean.

(All thanks to Akelard.)

"And this"—Carmen pushes a blushing Akelard forward— "is Akelard, our neighbour."

"Aw," coos Layla, her light brown eyes assessing his nervous posture. "Aren't you a cute little thing?"

"Ignore her." Omar rolls his eyes. "She seems to forget that you're eighteen years old."

"H—Hi," Akelard mutters shyly.

"So, I have a few movies," says Layla after they made themselves comfortable on the couches.

• • •

"Rewind that!" Adrian grins almost falling off the couch. "I want to see that scene again."

"We've watched that two times," Layla scowls. "What's so entertaining about Megan Fox undressing?"

"You won't know," Omar sighs dreamily and winces as Layla slaps his arm.

• • •

"*Why* are we watching this?" Carmen groans. "It's boring!"

"No it's not," Adrian replies indignantly. "*The Notebook* is one of the best books written by Nicholas Sparks. Of course, the movie does the book no justice but *still*, it's awesome!"

The room stills and Carmen smirks as Adrian's face flushes red. He coughs and scratches the back of his head. "What?"

"You read N—Nicholas S—Sparks?" Akelard scrunches his nose.

"Wow. That's new."

"What's wrong with reading Nicholas Sparks?" He raises an eyebrow. "It—his stories are cute, okay?"

"You're officially my new best friend," declares Layla as Omar snorts.

Adrian gives Layla a high five.

"Which is your favourite book, though?"

"The Notebook, of course! I don't really like The Choice, though."

Omar, Carmen and Akelard exchange weary looks as the newly paired 'best friends' discuss their favourite author's books.

"Let's do something other than this?" Carmen says, standing up. "Let's go up to the terrace."

"And do what?" Omar asks flatly.

"Talk something other than Nicholas Sparks and his racist books."

Cue in the glares from Adrian and Layla.

• • •

So, they decide to climb the stairs up to the terrace. Omar pushes opens the door which responds with a creaky sigh.

The view from the terrace is, as expected, heavenly. The five friends lay out a mat because the floor is dirty and they sit on it, folding their legs.

"Wow," Omar sighs. "This looks like a dream."

Stars twinkle down on them in agreement. Carmen can see Adrian's glazed eyes take in the sky. She knows how much he loves the stars. Back when they were in High School and he had had a bad night, he'd sneak her out to his house and take her up to his roof. There, seated against the slanting roof, he'd teach her the names of the stars and how he believed that when a person died, they would be a star.

And the ones who were the kindest would be the brightest star. Adrian believed that his mom was one of them.

"There aren't much stars in the c—cities," muses Akelard. "T—Trust me when I t—tell you that in the countryside, all you can s—see in the night sky are stars, stars and stars."

It isn't long before the boys divulge into the some other topic and the girls are discussing something else.

"He's a nice guy," mutters Layla, sneaking a look at Adrian who's chuckling at Akelard's red face. "You guys must be really good friends."

"We are," she says, "and we should've bought some wine up here."

"You don't say," Layla sighs. "Omar's family's coming this weekend."

Carmen narrows her eyes playfully. "You don't sound too happy."

"I'm not," she sighs, pushing her brown bangs away. "Omar's family doesn't really like me, anyway."

"Why?"

"They're pretty conservative. Omar's mom doesn't quite like me because I'm black," she chuckles darkly, "and atheist. She doesn't like that. Plus . . ."

"Hm?"

"Plus, I don't really have the best reputation around, y'know?"

Carmen cocks her head to the side. She can feel Omar looking at them and he probably knows that they're talking about him. "What do you mean?"

"Omar and I met when I was 17. I went through an abortion at that time." Layla closes her eyes and lets out a deep sigh. She opens her eyes and her caramel skin glints in the moonlight. "What do you think of that?"

"I don't know what to think," confesses Carmen. "Go on, though."

"Like I said, Omar's family don't like me and we're having dinner this week."

"Tough."

"Don't remind me."

So, when they leave, Carmen feels like the five of them are bound together with dark secrets and they were used to being shunned by society because of their flaws.

And yet each of them were *here*, laughing at Omar's lame puns because of their flaws. Jeroën, like always, was right.

"I mean, at the end, possessions will crumble, beauty will fade but . . . your flaws still stay with you, right? After all, they are a part of your inner beauty."

•••

Chapter 13

Carmen Chuckles Loudly

"You know how stupid this is? *I* have to invite *myself* over."

"No! I was about to but you kept interrupting me by babbling all about Lucia."

"Hmph, sure," grumbles Uncle Joe but Carmen can hear the amusement is his tone. "Anyways, Aunt Claudia's asking for you."

"What does she want?" Carmen asks distastefully.

"Careful with that tone, Cars. She wants you to come over for the weekend."

"No *way*."

"Carmen—" begins Uncle Joe.

"Let's be honest here, Uncle Joe. They'll call me there, insult me, make a fool out of me and that's it. I'm not going."

"You wouldn't do it for me?" Uncle Joe asks meekly.

"Are you — Oh, I get what you're doing, buddy." Carmen narrows her eyes.

"Please!" Uncle Joes laughs. "I'll be there and so will Lucy. We could go for fishing or something."

"I don't fish well, Uncle Joe."

"S'okay! I just want to see my niece. You'll come, right?"

Carmen sighs, rubbing the crease that's formed between her eyebrows. "Fine. It's not like I have a choice or something."

"Great! Um, I'll talk to Adrian and ell him to drop you near Emory Bridge. I'll pick you up from there."

• • •

"Where did Carmen go?"

Adrian clenches his jaw. "Out."

"Okay."

It's not that Adrian isn't trying because he really is but he just doesn't *get it* how anyone can make and easy conversation with *Death.*

"Do you want to watch this?" Adrian tries again, his green eyes twitching at the sight of Jeroën. His white hair's and dark black eyes are a complete contrast to his porcelain skin. He wonders how Carmen sees him.

"It does not matter, really." Jeroën shrugs. "You can put whatever you like."

• • •

ADRIAN: *where are you? How long is grocery shopping taking?*

ADRIAN: *Death boy's annoying the heck out of me with his stupid questions.*

ADRIAN: *He just asked me what the point of drinking alcohol was.*

ADRIAN: *WHAT KIND OF QUESTION IS THAT*

ADRIAN: *I just shrugged*

ADRIAN: *CARMEN*

CARMEN: *patience is virtue, my child.*

ADRIAN: *Can you come home quickly, pls? I can't tolerate him*

CARMEN: *i'll try. The queue's long*

CARMEN: *& be thankful, k? He sAvEd Ur lYf!*

ADRIAN: *you're being dramatic. Being sick is not synonymous to dying.*

CARMEN: *JUST GIVE HIM COMPANY*

ADRIAN: *Can I invite Akelard over?*

CARMEN: *don't be silly. Akelard's really scared of him.*

ADRIAN: *Ugh*

ADRIAN: *He's so boring, though.*

CARMEN: *gtg*

CARMEN: *be a good boy.*

CARMEN: *i raised u up like that. Don't do me shame, u hear?*

• • •

"Uh, you want something to eat, Jeroën?"

"I will have what you have." He smiles and Adrian cringes. "Can you describe how I look to you?"

"You don't know how you look?" Adrian raises his eyebrow in amusement.

"Well, I am not scared of myself, am I?"

"Fine. You have white hair. Like, striking white and you have really pale skin. You're tall and your eyes are like . . . a very dark black."

"Ah. So, I look bad?"

"You bet." Adrian closes the cabinet and takes out a bowl. He pours in a handful of popcorn and pushes it over to Jeroën. "Here. I don't really know what to make since we don't have much ingredients here. I hope you don't mind."

Jeroën shrugs. Adrian walks over to the counter and hoists himself up. He pops corn into his mouth and he swivels his tongue over it, relishing the taste. He takes his time with each corn. Anything to avoid looking at *him.*

He can feel Jeroën's black eyes on him. He feels insecure with the attention. He doesn't like it when his posture's too stiff around Jeroën.

"You are too intimidated by me."

". . ."

"I mean, you are too afraid of me. You are just . . . scared of everything, actually."

"Excuse me?" Adrian asks coldly.

"You are scared of me. You are scared of Death which pretty much sums it up. You do not want to accept reality—"

"Buddy," cuts in Adrian. "Don't talk about reality to me because we *all* know that there're people blasting their heads off and jumping off cliffs *because* of reality. *You* must know that," he laughs without any humour. "After all, you're Death."

Jeroën narrows his eyes. "I get that reality's too much to take in at times—"

"At *times?* I'll tell you what reality is, bud. It's that sinking realisation that no matter how many times you try to ignore all your past nightmares, they'll just keep haunting you. Reality's that . . . burden, some kind of shadow that everyone tries to avoid. Dreams are our way out. But what happens when you don't get any dreams? What happens if all you get are nightmares? Huh? You know . . . this whole bullshit theory of 'Life goes on' and shit? It does and that's the problem. Life goes on and it gives you doses of reality when we least need it."

"You sound like you are fed up of life."

"Isn't everybody?" Adrian's yelling now. His face is red with vehemence and his fingers are clawing the mahogany counter. "Isn't everybody fed up of life? I'd like to find one person who isn't. Everyone wants to enter some kind of oblivion which blocks them out from all the bad in this world" —he leans in closer— "everyone wants to get away from reality."

"I know what happened to you. So, I get why you're sour about it."

"What?" Adrian whispers hoarsely.

"About your mother—"

"How did you know?"

"I know everything. So, maybe you're afraid of reality, okay. I get that. Why are you afraid to accept that?

"Wha—what do you mean?" Adrian's tanned skin pales.

"I know you, Adrian Montague O'Connor. You're afraid of Death, reality . . . but I'll tell you what you're most afraid of." Jeroën stands up and strolls up to Adrian whose green eyes are trained on his porcelain face.

"You are afraid if people will not accept you for who you are. You are that kind of boy everyone loves and everyone aspires to be, right? You are that kind of boy who loves to chase the sun but when the night crawls in" —Adrian shivers as Jeroën leans in closer— "when the moon comes in and brings all your nightmares with it . . . that moment— that is who you really are, yes? A boy who is scared of what people think about him? A boy who pretends to be perfect but is far from it?"

"Get out."

"Sure. I get that you want your space—"

"*GET OUT!*"

Jeroën blinks impassively as Adrian's breathes out sharply in fury. He shrugs and leaves not before hearing the resounding crash of a glass bowl.

• • •

Chapter 14

Adrian's Having a Bad Day

Akelard gets that. He really does and he wishes everyone else could. As Melinda asks Adrian *another* question, Akelard expects to see smoke fuming from Adrian's ears.

"Thank you *so* much, Adriana—"

"*What?*"

"Uh, I—I was trying to give you a nickname," Melinda pales as Adrian glares at her.

"Oh right. Because my name's too long, right?"

"No. No. I—"

"You think it's amusing to call me a girl's name?"

"No, I—"

"Hey Adriana!"

If Adrian's head could explode from anger, it would. Hearing Sheila shout that out in a crowded corridor made him fume with anger even more.

Everybody laughs out. Adrian turns around, his eyes narrowed. Sheila's wearing a burgundy red dress with black tights and boots and she looks beautiful, as usual. If Adrian wasn't in such a resentful mood, he would've complimented her.

"What's up?" she winks.

"Nothing," he replies tautly. She cocks an eyebrow at his attitude.

Adrian hands Akelard his books and tells him to take it to class and that he would be there after a few minutes. He weaves himself out of the crowded corridor and finds himself seated on the bleachers.

It's windy and he's slightly grateful because he's sweating buckets in the heat.

"When the moon comes in and brings all your nightmares with it . . . that moment, that's who you really are, yes? A boy who's scared of what people think about him? A boy who pretends to be perfect but is far from it?"

"Damn you, Jeroën," he whispers, feeling tears prick his eyes. "Why do you have to be so right?"

"You okay there?"

Adrian's hand immediately reaches up to his face. He starts to rub the corners of his vigorously as though a dust particle is in his eye. "I'm fine."

I'm fine.

I'm fine.

I'm fine.

Am I really fine?

"No you're not." A wave of fresh smelling enchiladas washes over him. He wants that to be replaced with jasmines. He doesn't want Sheila. Right now, he wants Carmen. Carmen would listen. He doesn't have to be afraid of what Carmen would think of him.

"I am, really," he says and tries to smile. It turns out to be a grimace.

"Tell me what's wrong," she says. The kindness in her voice makes Adrian clench his jaw.

"Nothing."

"Come on. If you keep it in you, you're going to get angrier and—"

"Sheila, it's nothing, okay? I'm fine, I really am."

"Adrian—"

"Stop it!" he snaps and Sheila stills. "Just stop it, okay? Don't act like you're so worried. I'm not an idiot. I know about you. The whole Iudex thing" —Sheila's eyes widen— "and *I'm not an idiot*. So, stop acting like you care! Because at the end," he yells standing up, "you'll be *up there* and I'll be down *here* pretending to be *fine*. Just . . . leave me alone!"

• • •

"Adrian? Go get the door!"

Adrian shuts his laptop. He gets off the barstool and trudges all the way to the door and unlocks it before pulling it open. "Oh hey."

Akelard grins. He hands Adrian some books and says, "We have some sort of essay to write and hand in after two weeks. I've written what it's about in your journal and I've got you a few reference books to look into."

Adrian chuckles softly at his attempt to get him to smile. "Thanks bud. Come in."

"No, no," he rushes out. "I've got to start the essay. I have two essays to submit tomorrow."

"Okay, then. Have fun."

"You bet. Oh, and Adrian?"

"Yeah?"

"Uh, just . . . I mean," he blushes. "I—I if—"

"I thought you stopped stuttering around us," Adrian pouts. "Don't tell me you started again."

"If you want to talk or something, you can talk to me!"

Adrian raises his eyebrows. "I'm talking to you now, aren't I?"

"No, I mean—"

"I was messing with you," Adrian chuckles as Akelard glares at him. "Of course. I'll be better tomorrow. Promise."

"Okay," Akelard smiles. *"Du bist nicht die gleichen Adrian, wenn Sie sauer sind."*

"What does that mean?"

"What's the point of saying it in German if I'm going to translate it into English?"

"Get going, smartass."

Adrian shuts the door after he leaves and sticks his hands into the pockets of his beach pockets. He whistles some nursery tune and shuffles to the Carmen's room after placing the books on a table.

"What was it?" hums Carmen, scrawling something on her notebook.

"Oh, he just gave me a few books for my essay."

Carmen's red hair is tied into a bun and there's pencil stuck in there to support it. She's wearing a loose sweatshirt that makes her look like a stick in it. She veers her rolling chair around so that she's face to face with Adrian.

"I've been noticing you ever since I came back. You look . . . really off. What happened?"

"It's just," he sighs, ". . . Carmen, what if everyone's talking to me because they pity me?"

"Huh?"

"Yesterday," he swallows, "Jeroën told me that . . . I—that I'm afraid of how people think of me and . . . I just . . . it's actually true. He's right. I *am* afraid of other people's opinion about me. It scares me. Which makes me think . . . how many people know of this? How many just talk to me out of pity?"

"Adrian, stop."

"I— I can't, Cars. I can't go on like this. I can't lean on you for every single thing. I can't live with these nightmares accusing me for being a murderer. I can't pretend to be a happy-go-lucky guy. I can't pretend to be *cool.* I can't pretend to be *fine.* I can't pretend to be someone I'm not. I'm tired," he sighs, rubbing his eyes. "I'm just . . . bloody tired."

• • •

"Why are we up here?" he mutters, taking in their perimeter. It's not a starry night and that dampens Adrian's already dampened mood.

"I feel like this is our . . . venting spot."

"Venting spot?"

"Yup. I mean, in case I'm not there and you're pissed or in case you're not there and I'm pissed, we can just come up here and let it out. I trust the sun, the moon and the stars to keep our secrets," she winked.

"Carmen . . ."

"I kind of understand what you're going through but Adriana"— she chuckles as Adrian glares at her— "you have to toughen up. You're not the one only one in here wearing a mask. You don't have to pretend. I feel like I'm some kind of broken recorder who keeps repeating 'you don't have to pretend'. I keep telling that to you. Adrian, there's nothing wrong with fearing that people think of you. I swear to everything I own, there's nothing wrong with it."

"You wouldn't know," he mutters lowly.

"You're right. I don't but hey, I'm not complaining, right?" She ignores Adrian's glare. "Look, you're lucky that you have friends who don't exploit you for your flaws. There're so many people out there who wish to have friends like *me*—"

"Did you just . . . compliment yourself when you're supposed to be comforting *me*?"

"Aye, aye. I feel like not enough people compliment me. So, I have to do the deed."

"Right," he snorts. "You're on your way to modesty."

"Thanks Adriana. Your advice helps."

"Carmen!"

• • •

Chapter 15

Carmen Cocks an Eyebrow in Confusion

"Where's that?"

"Right across your street," Omar says lowering his voice as the professor scans the theatre for any sort of indiscipline.

"Why didn't you tell me this before?" she snaps. "I could've gotten you something."

"It's alright," he softly chuckles. "It really is. Just make sure that you, Adrian and Akelard come, okay?"

"Yeah, whatever," she huffs and draws another figure on her notebook. She looks up at the screen. "You'll be nineteen?"

"Duh." Omar rolls his eyes. "Remember, Flankton at seven, okay?"

"*Plankton*?" Carmen bites her lips to hold in the giggles. "What kind of restaurant name is that?"

"It's *Flank*ton," he grumbles. "The food is heaven, mind you."

• • •

"Ugh," he mutters as he looks around their vast library. Everyone's huddled around in groups, discussing their projects. Some of them wave at him and he waves back at them.

And then, he sees her.

Dodging a lot of chairs and tables, he finally reaches her table. Her legs are flung over a chair and a pencil's tucked in her ear.

"Hey."

Sheila looks up, startled. She visibly relaxes as she takes in the looming figure in front of her and gives him a soft smile. "Hey."

"Can I sit?"

"Sure," she says.

He pulls out a chair from a neighbouring table and sits on. He drums his fingers on the wooden table as she raises an eyebrow at his stiff posture. "You okay there?"

Adrian feels a wave of déjà-vu wash over him and guilt strikes him. "I'm sorry for . . . yesterday."

"It's okay," she sighs. "I mean, it's pretty impressive that you believed it."

"It took a lot of time," he smiles. "Jeroën wasn't very helpful."

"Can't blame him," she laughs. "He *is* a Death, after all. He's pretty blind to everyone's feelings."

"Figures," he mutters. "But I really am sorry for my behaviour yesterday. I was just . . . really brash."

"You were," she hums. "But it's alright."

They sit in silence, Adrian takes out a few of his books and Sheila pushes away a few of her books to give him space. He opens up his books and starts to write his essays.

When he feels that she's not looking at him, he looks up. He discreetly watches how her blonde ringlets fall over her eyes. He smiles softly when her brown eyes narrow in annoyance and how she pinches the bridge of her nose when she doesn't get something right.

"Done staring at my beautiful face?"

"Sure," he mutters, hastily looking at his book. "Hey, Sheila?"

"Yeah."

"Jeroën told me about . . . how you and your father are in a row because you wanted to stay here. What's so special here?"

She lays her pencil down and looks up. Her dark brown eyes crinkle up as she smiles. "What isn't so special here?"

"I hate it when people do that."

"Do what?"

"When you answer a question with a question. It's cryptic and annoying."

She chuckles softly. Adrian grins at that. He likes listening to her laugh.

"I just . . . I guess I was being optimistic. Father had thought that as soon as I would come to Earth, I'd see all the wrong things and I'd come back but I saw all the good things."

"Like what?"

Sheila gawks at him in disbelief. "Come on, Adrian! There're so many things to love here! You've lived here. Maybe that's why you don't find much but I guess you'd understand if you stayed in Purgatory."

"What's . . . Purgatory like?"

"It's . . . dark. The place is filled with agony obviously and it's . . . just, I mean the whole place echoes with screaming and shouting—"

"Why?"

"People get rid of their sins," says Sheila. "It's like emptying your soul from everything. From all your sins and sins . . . they're plastered to your soul. So, cleansing you from your sins can be pretty painful."

"But . . . pain is an emotion," Adrian says slowly, "and that's a part of the human body so . . ."

"It's not . . . *painful*," she says contorting her face. "It's hard to explain but if you say so, how's hell supposed to be bad? If pain is a part of human body then hell's just another place, right?"

"That's really if you believe in it."

"That's it," she says smiling. "Everything depends on perception. Just like Death. It's how you perceive things. Like Death, you see?"

Adrian sighs, "Wow."

"Ha, you tell me."

• • •

"Get. Up!"

"I don't want to go!" Adrian whines, covering his head with his covers. "I'm really sleepy."

"So am I," scowls Carmen. "But look at me. Come on!"

"It's just . . ." Adrian sneaks a look at the clock hanging on the wall opposite to his bed, "three! He said it's at . . . seven, right? Why would I wake up *now*?"

"Because we have to get him gifts!" She groans, pulling his hand. "Get up!"

"Okay!" he exclaims. He runs his eyes that are groggy from tiredness and squints at the figure leaning on the doorway.

"Hey, you're coming with us, Akelard?"

"Yup," he grins. "Get dressed, now."

"Wait, wait," Adrian says. "Which restaurant is it, again?"

"Flankton."

"Sounds very interesting. It sounds so good that I don't want to go."

"You're getting up in three seconds."

"You'll make a bad wife," he retorts.

"One." Carmen holds up a finger.

"Wait, are you serious?"

"Two."

"Okay, okay, I'm going!" He says trying to get up but ends up tripping on the covers and falling back to bed.

"Three."

WHACK.

Adrian looks at the red handprint on his shoulder in disbelief. He looks up at Carmen who's mimicking his expression.

"You're a dead woman."

And the apartment is filled with Akelard's laughs as he watches the two best friends chase each other, shouting profanity and throwing things at each other.

• • •

"Adrian," hisses Carmen. "*Why* are you in the lingerie section?"

"Do you *have* to ask?"

"Get going!" she says slapping his arms — a little too hardly.

"Hey!" he scowls. "You're so lucky you're a girl . . . but," he grins impishly, "I'm all for gender rights" — he cracks his knuckles playfully— "so, I'd watch my actions if I were you."

"*Oooh*," she says sarcastically, holding up her hands in mock surrender. "I'm shivering with fear!'

"Can I help you please?"

Adrian turns to the direction of the sweet voice and finds a short woman looking up at them expectantly.

"Uh, no—" starts Carmen.

Adrian holds up his hand. "My friend here thinks that none of these bras will fit her."

The lady looks at Carmen sympathetically. "Well, we can size you up—"

"No, no!" rushes Carmen, already making plans on how to execute Adrian's murder. "I'm fine, thank you. I'll call you if I need you, okay?"

She smiles and walks up to another girl, repeating the same question.

"You," she frowns," are dead to me."

"What a—are y—you two d—doing here?"

Adrian clenches his jaw as he looks at the person behind Carmen. "Akelard, I told you to stay with me. Why do you keep running away?"

"Th—that's because you wouldn't come with me!" he says. "I figured that Omar would want some Xbox games because . . . he a— always talks about his Xbox—"

"See?" says Carmen, placing her hands on her hips. "Now, why don't you go with Akelard and pick out a few games?"

"Fine," he grumbles. Grabbing Akelard's hand, he says to him, "Now, you stick to me, okay? I know how you don't like crowds. So, don't leave, okay?"

Akelard blushes and nods quickly.

• • •

"Carmen! That shirt looks awesome!"

"I thought boys didn't like pink? Adrian, I swear to God, if this is some kind payback —"

"Omar *loves* pink."

Carmen looks at Akelard who takes a sudden interest in his shoes.

"Okay . . ."

"You're welcome."

• • •

"Okay," sighs Adrian, arranging his hair. "Now all we have to do is find them."

Carmen rolls her eyes. Standing the midst of a crowded expensive looking restaurant and trying to find Omar and Layla wasn't exactly easy.

"Why does everyone looks so . . . sophisticated over here?" Akelard asks meekly. His hair is combed back neatly and he's wearing an odd neon blue jacket that looks really weird because it has white tassels hanging down from the shoulder blades. Carmen had tried to change his mind but he was adamant.

"Nah, you just look extra weird," says Adrian with a smirk.

"Hey!"

"Guys," says Carmen interrupting the pair. "I found them. Let's go."

The trio walks over to the table in the corner after dodging a lot of people. Carmen stretches her back and hears a satisfying crack because it's not easy to sidestep couple who are intent on sticking their butts out and leaning across too tables to give their lovers a kiss instead of just *sitting* and *eating.*

"Hey!" Omar smiles as they take their seats. "You guys made it. I was wondering if you guys stood me up."

Adrian sighs dramatically. "Well, it's not like we had a choice."

Layla throws a napkin at him which he darts away from.

"This restaurant looks lovely, Omar," Carmen smiles.

"You're supposed to be saying that *I* look good," he whines childishly getting them to laugh. "Hey, Akelard?"

"Y—yeah?"

"Not that you look bad or anything but your jacket's kind of . . . hurting my eyes. Could you take it off?"

Akelard scowls and opens his mouth to retort but Layla beats his to it by saying, "God, Akelard. That jacket looks *horrible*. Where did you get that hideous jacket from?"

"My aunt gave this to me for Hanukkah!"

"Well, you shouldn't have worn it here. People are staring, Akelard," says Adrian, taking a sip of his water.

"I don't care," he says haughtily. "I think it looks splendid."

"Well, Omar," says Adrian, wiping a fake tear. "You're nineteen, bro."

"No shit, Captain Obvious."

"It's time you started acting like one, though."

Before Omar can tell Adrian exactly what he thinks of him, Adrian shoves his gift across the table.

Omar glares at him and proceeds to rip the wrapping — quite violently.

"Dude," says Omar and he looks up. His eyes are shining as he coughs out, "Y—You got me the newest Xbox games! I—I—" he blubbers, "I love you."

"I don't really bat for that team, man."

"You're ruining the mood."

By the time, Omar unwraps Akelard's present, he's an emotional ball.

"I love you too," he sniffs. Carmen raises an eyebrow at him because he's actually crying.

"O—Okay." Akelard blushes furiously.

Layla pretends to be offended but Omar gives her kisses which make the three single friends stare bitterly at the couple.

It seems like an eternity is over when Omar pulls away. Layla's coloured cheeks are identical to Akelard's. Omar claps his hands. "Okay, Carmen. Bring it on."

"..."

"..."

"Uh . . ." Omar swallows. "This is . . . nice."

"Wait. You don't like pink shirts?" Carmen asks.

Omar glares at Adrian. "You promised me you wouldn't tell anyone."

"Sorry," Adrian says blankly.

"All I can feel is betrayal."

"I feel cold. When's the waitress coming here?"

"I trusted you."

"Huh, really? Hey, how is the sushi over here?"

"I hate you."

"Could've *sworn* you said the exact opposite a minute ago."

"Well, I hate you now."

"My heart's breaking."

"Of *course*, he like pink," Layla cuts in. "He wears pink pyjamas with white polka dots on it."

"Hey, it doesn't have polka dots!"

"*Sure.*"

Throughout the evening, Adrian finds himself thinking about Sheila and Carmen finds herself thinking about Jeroën as they watch two of their friends in love.

• • •

Chapter 16

Adrian is Anything but Happy

"Are you sure you can manage?"

". . ."

"Adrian," sighs Carmen. "It's just for one day. You drop me there today. I'll spend tomorrow there and I'll come the day after."

"It's easy for you to say that," he says, stopping at a red signal. "Why are you going there? All they'll do is just . . . teasing you."

"Uncle Joe will be there," she says, tucking a strand behind her ear.

"You could've invited him here," he says pointedly.

Carmen stares at him flatly. "Adrian."

"Okay," he frowns. "I'm being selfish but . . . Carmen, *one* day."

"I'll call you," she chuckles. "Don't worry, okay?"

"Fine," he grumbles. "Just . . . put on the radio or something."

His Toyota Prius that his dad had gifted him for his seventeenth birthday, trudges along the highway with some classic Mariah Carey blasting through the speaker.

As he drives, he thinks how he's going to survive the *night*. He doesn't want to go through that alone.

"Okay," she says softly. "That's Emory Bridge."

He spots a familiar black Range Rover parked on the side, so he slows down his car and parks in front of it.

The door opens and Adrian grins as Uncle Joe steps out. Carmen rushes out of the door and into his arms, squealing loudly.

He gets the key out of its ignition and pockets it before getting out of the car.

Uncle Joe smiles, and holds out his arms for Adrian as well. Adrian chuckle loudly and allows himself to be embraces by him. He inhales his Hawaiian coconut smell and an infinite number of sweet memories rush into his head and he almost wishes to not have left home with Carmen.

"Look at you," he grins after they pull away. "You've grown taller."

"*Sure.*" He rolls his eyes.

"Hey, Steven said he's in Baker's Inn for some kind of meeting and since that's close by so you can meet up with him."

"Why's dad—oh right. Meeting." He nods. "Where's Baker's Inn again?"

After Uncle Joe gives the directions, he gives Adrian another hug before getting into his jeep.

"Call me as soon as you get there, alright?"

"Okay," she says softly and they hug.

Jasmines. Jasmines. If only this could keep my nightmares away.

They pull away and he gives her a charming smile. "Bye."

● ● ●

"Dad?"

Steven looks up from his plate of pancakes. "Adrian! You're here!"

"Yeah," he smiles and slides into the seat opposite to his father's.

"Joe told me that you might be here," he says.

"Yup. I just drove Carmen. This place is pretty hard to find," Adrian hums looking around the cosy restaurant.

"Is it?"

"Can I take your order, please?"

Adrian looks up and smiles at the girl. "Uh, yeah. We'll have pancakes with honey."

"So," his dad grins. His eyes are green—just like his. "How's college?"

"You ask me this whenever we call." Adrian fishes out his phone and places it on the table. "My opinion about college won't change in a month, dad."

"Your mother would've been so proud of you," his father says softly.

He doesn't respond. Instead, he feels *weak*. He remembers her blonde straight hair. He remembers how she used to ruffle his mess of curls. He remembers how she used to place a note in his lunch box every day telling him how much she loved him.

He remembers it all.

He remembers *that* day. Her pleas. Her cries. It's echoing through his head and he shuts his eyes immediately hoping that the memory wouldn't flash before his eyes.

He hasn't gone to her grave in years. He had only gone to it once and that was at her funeral and ever since that day he made it a point to never go with Carmen when she visited her dad and brother because he always felt like the letters of his mom's name *swirled* and on that day, the letters had rearranged from *Louisa Macheck O'Connor* to *Murderer.*

He's not a murderer.

"Here's your order." A plate of fresh smelling pancakes and honey wafts by his nostrils and a smile finds its way to his lips.

"Hey, Adrian?"

"Yeah dad?"

Steven grins widely. "So, is there a girl?"

"No," he says flatly.

"Really? Maybe . . . a Sheila?"

"God! Why do you talk to Carmen more than you talk to me?" He shoves a forkful of pancake dipped in honey into his mouth.

"Because she has more than 'nothing much' to say to me."

Adrian guffaws.

"So, do you like this girl?"

He thinks of her blonde hair, her warm brown eyes, her laugh and just *everything* about her. "Yeah. I guess I do."

"Well then? Why don't you tell her?"

"She's not like us— I mean, she's already in love with someone else," he says quickly, gulping down water.

• • •

"I wanted to invite Adrian too," sighs Uncle Joe, "but Claudia was against it."

"Why are you guys so afraid of her?" she snickers.

"She's just . . . so bossy and intimidating. Lucia hates her."

Carmen sinks down the leather seat. "I'm looking forward to this weekend."

"Hey, look on the bright side! We could go fishing and . . ."

"Fishing," Carmen deadpans. "You know how I suck at fishing."

"I do. That's why I suggested it."

Carmen slaps his arm playfully. His blue eyes twinkles as he tells her, "Lauren's been asking about you the whole time."

"Lauren!" gaps Carmen. "Gosh, I feel so guilty. I haven't called her in like . . . ages!"

"Yeah, she's pretty excited to see you."

She grins as she thinks about her twelve year old cousin. "Yeah, I can say the same 'bout her. How's she?"

"Fine, I guess. You should see her paintings, Cars. It's real gold. She's going to be a great artist if she swings that way. But of course"—he rolls his eyes— "*they* think it's too below their standard."

"No way."

"Last Sunday, you should've seen the row they made because she painted instead of having dinner with some hotshot lawyer's family."

"Ouch," she cringes. "That sucks."

They drive in silence for a while. Uncle Joe's humming to some song but all that's in Carmen's head is Jeroën, Jeroën and Jeroën.

• • •

"You killed me. You killed me. I had dreams, son. So many dreams but you ruined it all. We could've been a happy family. We could've been everything you ever wanted . . ."

"I . . . no . . ."

"I wanted to live too! You're so selfish—"

He opens his eyes, gasping for breath. He sits up, his back against the headboard and he pulls his knees up to his chest, weeping endlessly.

He wants to call her. He wants to call Carmen. He wants her to tell him that it's okay and yet, he doesn't want to feel so dependent on her.

So, Adrian reaches out to his nightstand, switches on the lamp and detaches his phone from its charger.

He calls Sheila.

• • •

Chapter 17

Carmen Clenches Her Fist

"And you look so skinny! I thought Adrian was a good cook!"

"He is," forces out Carmen. "I just don't eat that much."

"Nowadays," sighs Uncle Adam, letting out a puff of smoke from his mouth, "girls tend to get really afraid of a little flab."

"But, our Carmen," Aunt Claudia smirks maliciously, "is *fearless*."

The den echoes with laughter as Carmen turns red. She curls her sweaty palms into a fist.

"Well, well, I'm tired. Let's go to sleep."

Her aunts, uncles and cousin leave Uncle Joe's house. That's the things about her mom's family. They lived in the same neighbourhood and it would've been great only if she actually liked them.

"Ignore them," says Uncle Joe with a smile.

She scowls at him and without bothering to say a 'hey' to Lucia who stares at her expectantly, she trudges up the stairs to her room.

She pushes open the door and that feeling of . . . *home* flushes over her. She looks around her room, silently savouring the pale blue colour on the walls. She chuckles softly as she remembers how Adrian used to slip in through her large French windows when he used to have bad nights and how he used to sneak her out just watch the sunset.

She misses it.

Carmen traipses to her bed and plops down on it. Before she can take out her laptop, her eyes fall on the photo of her father, her mother and a two year old Carmen seated on a pew, all chuckling. That photo was taken before Ben was born.

"Oh mom," sighs Carmen, brushing her finger through her mother's smiling face. "How did you *live* with such sisters?"

When she was young, her dad used to make her and her brother sit near the fireplace and he'd tell them their mom's family's story.

Her mom was born in a very rich family. Carmen's grandparents used to be rich and successful doctors until someone put some kind of poison into the medicines.

So, all that richness and success went down the drain.

They had decided to move into a town where the expenses were low. Carmen's dad, Grant Collins had come all the way from Germany to settle down in America and look for a job.

And *that* was how her parents met.

Of *course*, her dad had never told her *how* they met each other but Carmen strongly suspected it to be a one night stand considering the fact how she was born two years before they were married and how her family—from her mother's side hated her dad so much.

• • •

"It's horrible! I hate it here."

"Aw man. You should've come next week."

"Why?" Carmen raises her eyebrows. "What's the difference?"

Markus grins cheekily at her. "I would've been there. Mom called me to come next week."

"Oh," she frowns, scratching her chin. "You should've told me that before. Anyways, this sucks."

Markus reaches out for something, probably beside the laptop and the camera shakes a bit so his image is wavering for a few seconds.

"It's just for like . . . one day, right? You'll be back in Cali in no time."

"Still," she persists. "It's going to go bad."

She looks up as she hears her door creak, Lucia's blonde head peeks in and she smiles at her.

"Hey, I gotta go. I'll call you back later, okay?"

"Okay."

She shuts the laptop and smiles brightly at Lucia who grins back at her. "Sorry. I was in a bad mood."

"I wouldn't blame you. But sitting and talking on Skype for the whole night is pretty sad." she says in her Spanish accent before sauntering in. Lucia plops down on the bed and leans in. "Hey, you want to come to the beach with me?"

Carmen looks at her window and squints as the sun shines brightly at her. "Okay. Is it just you and me or is Uncle Joe coming along?"

"Just you and me."

•••

The sun kisses the sea and it gives a nice blue glow to the water as the waves wash over Carmen's feet. She crinkles her toes feeling the water tickle her feet.

"How was Paris?" she says loudly. Lucia looks up at her and says, "Heavenly. Especially when you're there on your honeymoon and when you're in love."

Carmen chuckles and walks back to the shore with Lucia. She flattens out her floral dress before sitting on the picnic mat.

"I'm sorry about how they treated you," Lucia cringes, uncorking her bottle of orange juice. She takes a sip and lets out a sigh. "It's just so . . . grousing of them."

"Usually, I wouldn't bother," says Carmen. "It's just . . . I've kind of forgotten about them and coming back here . . . everything—like, my old life—life before college, it just hit me. How could I just . . . forget everything?" she laughs weakly.

"I would forget them if I could," snorts Lucia. "When I stepped into your Aunt Claudia's house, she wouldn't look my way."

"Why?" asks Carmen. She opens her beach basket and takes out a burger wrapped in foil. She tears off the foil and takes a huge bite.

"You don't know?"

"Know what?"

"About my . . . problem . . ."

Carmen cocks an eyebrow. "What problem?"

"About my infertility," Lucia says and looks away quickly.

Carmen crumbles the foil and dusts away the grains of the bread that has fallen on her floral dress.

"Before you say anything," Lucia says quickly. "Your uncle knew about this before we . . . got married."

"Okay," chuckles Carmen. "I wasn't going to say anything so relax. I'm sorry about my aunts, though. They're just crazy."

"I know." Lucia sighs sadly. "Your uncle really wanted kids."

"Yeah," Carmen says, staring into the sunset. Adrian would've loved to be here. "He did. Two boys and one girl."

"Hey, it's getting quite late. Your uncle must be home by now. Let's go."

So, as Lucia begins to pack everything up and as much as Carmen wants to *deny* it, she discreetly checks her out.

Of *course*, it wasn't checking out. It was more like . . . observing her.

Carmen had always thought that it was utter stupidity that Lucia wanted to work as a primary teacher than to work as a model because her long and lean figure which was complimented with her suave curves looked perfect.

Or in Adrian's way of putting it through, her body was *killin'* it.

• • •

"Carmen?"

Carmen gasps almost dropping her phone. She turns her rolling chair around and visibly relaxes when she sees Lauren.

"Laur. Gee, you scared me."

Lauren grins showing her white teeth. She steps inside and closes the door softly behind her.

"You didn't come yesterday," Carmen says raising her eyebrows. "Why didn't you join your mom and da—"

"Stepdad," she corrects curtly. She strolls over to Carmen's bed and plops on it. "You sad you'd call me when you reach there."

"You said you'd call me too," Carmen retorted childishly. "I missed you, Laur."

"Me too, Cars. I missed you too. I just want to"—she lets out a deep sigh— "run away from here. Run away from all of them."

"Come on, it can't be that bad."

"You don't understand, Cars." Lauren looks at her with her sparkling brown eyes. Her blonde frizzy hair is tied into a pony tail and she's wearing a floral dress like she usually does. "Mom's completely changed after she met that guy."

Carmen wants to agree with her but she doesn't want Lauren to blossom any kind of hate towards Lauren's stepdad. She remembers noticing that about Aunt Rose, Lauren's mother. She was someone who was kind and accepting unlike her other aunts. Right now, she felt that Aunt Rose was sophisticated with her head stuck in her husband's riches.

"Don't say that, Laur. You're just afraid to let one person in."

"No, I'm not!"

Carmen rolls her eyes. "Not everyone's like Zed, dummy."

Lauren blushes red.

If Carmen could cite one childhood romance story, she's pick out Lauren and Zed's story over anything. She smiles crookedly as the image of the brunette boy flashes in her head.

Alas, like most childhood romances *start*, Zed had to leave to Washington leaving poor old Lauren to weep in her seclusion.

"Shut up," she grumbles. "You suck."

"Tsk, tsk," grins Carmen. "That's no way to speak to your cousin who's—might I add—*six* years older than you."

"Where's Adrian?" Lauren asks immediately.

"Back in Cali. Speaking of Adrian, I need to call him."

"Is this my cue to leave?"

"Aye." Carmen points at the door. "There's the door. You may leave."

"You're way too subtle in kicking people out," snorts Lauren, brushing back a blonde curl.

"It's my speciality," she winks.

• • •

"So, basically, you guys talked about demons?"

"And blood sucking vampires," adds Adrian quite excitedly. "It was awesome!"

"I don't get it," sighs Carmen. "Usually guys retort to sex talks to get a girl. You talked about demons to Sheila?"

"She initiated the whole topic, okay? Anyways, what really matters is that I slept yesterday."

"So, you don't need me anymore," she says pretending to be offended. "I get it."

"Well, that's what you get for leaving me here," he chuckles.

"I wish I didn't. You should've been here. There's a total riot goin' on here."

"What do you mean?"

"Dunno. All my aunts are fighting over something related to— money, obviously and it's super uncomfortable to be seated among middle aged aunts and uncles who don't talk at all."

"My family's way better than yours. Period."

"Thanks."

"Hey . . ." Adrian says softly and Carmen has to press her ear to the phone to hear him. "You'll be here tomorrow, right?"

"That's only if you pick me up from when Uncle Joe drops me."

Carmen can imagine Adrian rolling his eyes. "I will, Carmen. Of course, I will."

"So, hey, what were you doing the whole day besides completing your essays?"

"Hey man!" Adrian shouts and Carmen cringes. She can hear the door's creak and a few claps until Adrian says, "Hey Cars, I have to go."

"Okay, bye. Be there tomorrow by nine, okay?"

"Bingo. Oh, and Carmen?"

"Yeah?"

"You were right. Jeroën's not a bad guy."

"Wait what?"

Beep, beep, beep.

• • •

Chapter 18

Adrian Stares at Jeroën's Arm in Odd Fascination

He props his head on his arm and sits up, leaning against the headboard. Jeroën's pursing his lips as he stares at Adrian's laptop in confusion.

Adrian doesn't know whether he's supposed to feel disgusted or sorry at the amount of names that appears and vanishes in a matter of seconds. The names were scrawled on his hand in black italics and it just *appeared* and *vanished*.

Wendy.

Allen.

Ahmed.

"Do you ever . . . you know, feel anything when these names just like come and go?"

"No," Jeroën says blankly. "If I did, then I would be human."

"Oh, what I meant was, do you feel anything in terms of physical plain? Because these names just . . . dissolve into your skin."

Jeroën flicks his white hair from his forehead and shakes his head. "No. I do not feel a thing."

"And this . . . why do you get this? Is it some kind of reminder that you're Death?" Adrian asks.

Jeroën laughs loudly ignoring Adrian's immature scowl. "It is like . . . okay. Like how you are a human and how breathing is a necessity. That is how it is with me."

"Oh," Adrian says dumbly. "Right. So, it's there in all of you guys?"

"Yes."

"Another question: Do you feel any kind of remorse when you take people's souls away?"

"No," Jeroën snorts. "'Course not. Why do you think I am called Death?"

"Oh. Right. You must think I'm an idiot," Adrian laughs weakly.

"Huh, yes, I do."

"Whatever. Do you want to come with me to pick up Carmen?"

"Sure, yes."

"Why can't you just say 'yeah'?"

"Because I cannot."

"Why can't you just say 'can't'?"

"For *Christ's sake,* shut up!"

• • •

"Jeroën, just switch it off!" Adrian says annoyed. Jeroën's been fiddling with the radio ever since they got into his car. "Just do me a favour and look out for a black Range Rover that has—oh hey! There they are!"

Adrian grins widely as he pulls over at the Emory Bridge. He can see Carmen leaning over the railings that overlooked a vast sea.

"It's too early to die, Cars!" Adrian says as he rushes out of his car. Carmen turns around quickly and grins. She leans back and props her elbows on the railing.

"Took you some time, Adrian."

"You can thank your friend," Adrian says and points at his car. Carmen looks at the car and raises a sceptical eyebrow as Jeroën waves weakly at her.

"What's going on?"

"What do you mean?"

"What do you mean by 'what do you mean'? You know what I mean!"

Adrian smiles sheepishly. "Maybe I do."

They stare at each other. Blue eyes versus green eyes.

"This is the part when you tell me what's going on," Carmen states.

"Hey Adrian!"

Adrian smiles as he spots Uncle Joe walking towards him. "Oh hey."

"You were taking forever so I thought that I'd just take a walk."

"Huh, sorry about that. Now that I'm here . . ."

Uncle Joe makes a shooing motion with his hand.

• • •

"So, yesterday, Jeroën dropped here because he thought you'd be here."

"Aw. How sweet of him."

"You don't say. Anyways, he came in and I was in a pretty sour mood because—"

"Because I wasn't there?" Carmen asks with a teasing smile.

"Don't get your hopes too high," he mutters. "I was in a pretty sour mood and he sort of . . . demanded me to make him breakfast. Now I don't know about you but he scares the freaking shit out of me."

"I'm not scared. Remember about me being fearless?" Carmen asks sarcastically. She shakes her head t him and opens the zip of her suitcase.

Adrian flushes red before nibbling on his lip. "Sorry."

"S'okay. Continue."

"Yeah, anyways. I gave him breakfast and then Sheila calls me." A dreamy smile finds its way on his face. "And I might've talked about her for hours to Jeroën after the call—"

"No way. You didn't actually talk about your crush on the daughter of Iudex to a Death?"

"It sounds grave when you put it that way," Adrian frowns.

"That's because it *is* grave!"

"Do you want to hear what happened or not?"

"Sorry. Continue."

"*And*, Jeroën actually told me everything about her!"

"Oh. Kay."

"Thought you'd be a bit enthusiastic," he grumbles.

"I just—what did he tell you?" she asks and starts to pull out her clothes from her suitcase.

"Like what she likes and what she dislikes. Basically, with all the information I have, I might have a chance to make her my girlfriend!"

•••

Carmen bites her lip as she shuffles around the kitchen, shutting and opening the cabinets, looking for the right ingredients.

"I don't really know what to make. What do you want?"

She waits for Jeroën's response and when she doesn't get it, she huffs wearily. Before she can turn around, Jeroën has himself pressed against her and his arms are resting on the wooden counter.

Carmen's eyes widens to the size of saucers as she feels his breath fan her hair.

"I . . . wha . . ."

"I do not know," he whispers huskily. "But I will have what you will have."

And then, Carmen feels a flush of cold air unravel her back as Jeroën moves away. He catches her by her elbow and turns her around so that she's facing him. Now that she's looking at Jeroën's handsome face and his red lips and his define eyebrows and his long eyelashes and his long nose, she feels dizzy all over again.

"How was that?!"

"Huh . . . what . . ." Carmen can't form a proper sentence.

"That. That" —Jeroën screws his eyebrows together— "thing I did there! Did you feel . . . hmmm, what is that word he told me? Aha! Turned on. Did you feel turned on?"

Carmen chokes on her spit. "Did you just say what I think you said?"

"Did you think I said something along the lines of getting turned on?"

"Yes!"

"Voila! I *just* said that!"

"Oh my God!" gawks Carmen, blushing. "You're crazy!"

"Did you get turned on?"

Carmen stares at him incredulously. "That's . . . you can't ask me that!"

Jeroën smiles triumphantly and raises his head a bit. "You did!"

"How can you say that?"

"Because Adrian told me how girls acts very flustered after they get turned on."

"Stupid asshole," she mutters. "Don't spend too much time with him."

Jeroën leans in loser and Carmen finds herself trapped between him and the edge of the counter again. She places her hands on his strong chest and tries to push him but he doesn't budge.

"Why? Are you jealous?"

And then, he steps two steps back and smiles as though he won a lottery. "You got turned on again!"

"Don't say such things out loud!"

"Why not?"

"And I thought I wouldn't be giving the sex talk until I got kids," Carmen says darkly.

• • •

"Stop shivering," says Carmen feeling amused. "He's not going to kill you." *I hope.*

Akelard smiles weakly at Jeroën who smiles widely at him. He seems happier now. "He just gives off this evil enigma that I feel like pulling out that cross chain on your neck and shoving it on his face."

"You wouldn't," scoffs Carmen. "You'd faint before any of that."

Adrian laughs before taking a swing of his beer. He nudges Carmen and says, "Why don't you go and sit next to him? He looks pretty lonely."

The four of them were seated in the balcony, eating pork chops and drinking beer. Since Akelard was super scared of Jeroën (which Jeroën found highly amusing), Jeroën sat against the railing, sipping his beer.

Carmen gets up from the floor and flattens out her floral skirt. She walks gingerly over to him and sits next to him.

"Heya."

"Hello," he smiles, twirling a flower in his hand.

"Where did you get that from?"

"You have a pot of these flowers in your bathroom."

"Oh."

Jeroën chuckles. He looks at her thoughtfully and then, he looks away with a small smirk.

"You look very beautiful."

Carmen swallows thickly and chuckles weakly. "Yeah?"

"Yes. You should wear these kind of . . . floral dresses more. You look like . . . elegance and beauty combined."

"That's an awfully romantic thing to say."

"Thank you! I was really trying to be! Adrian said that even if I looked ugly to most people, I might have a shot at getting a girl."

Carmen quirks her lips feeling amused. "Is that what you want?"

"Adrian said that I'd feel more human and less Death if I did that."

"I thought that that was bad. I thought you came here to feel the opposite."

"Feeling and being are two different things, Carmen."

They sit in silence, drinking their beer and listening to Adrian and Akelard bicker about something insignificant.

"Have I told you about what happened in 1500?"

Carmen shakes her head. "Nope."

"You see, the Authority is really paranoid about any Death having feelings because . . . we have the power to take people's souls away and when we start to have feelings like love, hate and whatever, we get more powerful."

"Okay."

"In 1500, a Death was sent down to Earth because" —he points at himself— "like me, he was starting to lose interest in what he was doing. He was sent down and after some time, he fell in love with the daughter of a Count and when a Death falls in love—"

"He or she gets more powerful," completes Carmen.

"Yes. So, the Authority bought him back to Purgatory and tortured him—"

"Sorry, but how do you torture a Death? I thought you guys were immune to feelings."

"Oh, Carmen." Jeroën rolls his eyes. "I told you about how much of a delicate being a Death is. When he or she falls in love, you are exposed to everything. To all kinds of feelings. Be it hate, lust or anything. You are more porous to feelings when you fall in love. When Iudex—no,

Percontator, tortures a Death, he removes all feelings from a Death which means, he's ripping out a soul that is starting to form."

"Ah," Carmen says slowly, "and what about that girl? What about that girl he fell in love with?"

Jeroën shrugs nonchalantly. "She committed suicide after a year or two, I think."

Carmen shudders involuntarily. "Has this happened before? I mean, has anything similar happened after the 1500 incident."

"Maybe but I was not there then. But ever since the 1500 incident, there have been no cases of such."

She takes a sip from her beer and suddenly, she feel like it's bitterer. "That's . . . quite complicated."

Jeroën lifts the flower gingerly to his nose and takes a delicate sniff of it. He closes his eyes for a brief second, almost like he's committing the smell of the flower to his memory. He looks at Carmen and Carmen thinks that his grey eyes look brighter than usual.

"Maybe," he whispers and tucks the flower behind Carmen's ear. He brushes back a few strands of her red hair and says, "I feel like saying the same things again and again will reduce the meaning of it."

"What do you mean?" she swallows.

"You look very beautiful."

• • •

Chapter 19

Carmen Has Birds Tweeting Cheerily in Her Head

"You're acting like you won a lottery," says Adrian suspiciously. He sits across Carmen and taps his fingers on the counter.

"Maybe I did."

Adrian narrows his eyes as she grins widely and pours milk into her glass.

"Oh wait."

"What?"

"You're happy because," he laughs, "Jeroën called you beautiful? *Really?*"

"No!" she says blushing furiously. "Don't be stupid."

"*I'm* being stupid? You're the one getting all flustered because he said that you were beautiful."

"Pfft. I'm not flustered."

". . ."

"Your *stop-shitting-me* look is not going to change my answer."

"..."

"Okay! Fine. I'm a bit . . ."

"Carmen," Adrian says looking amused. "Don't tell me that you have a crush on him."

"What if I do?" she says in a challenging voice.

"Oh. My. *Gaaad*," he says dramatically.

"Oh, shut up."

"You have *got* to be kidding me! That's practically impossible."

"I know," she says softly. "It's not like it would be any different if he was not Death."

Adrian looks at her flatly. "Carmen, you're amazing."

Carmen sniffs wiping a fake tear from the corner of her eye. "Thanks, Adrian."

"Don't let anyone tell you otherwise."

"Thing is, they don't."

"Wa—hey! Look at you, being modest and shit."

• • •

His hair is the softest thing she has ever touched.

Jeroën's black hair was all tousled by the end of their CAD period because Carmen would 'accidentally' slide her book all the way over to Jeroën's table and she would reach out and 'accidentally' brush her fingers through his hair.

"Why are you looking at me like that?" Jeroën asks quirking an eyebrow as they walk down a corridor.

"Like what?"

"Like" —he makes a heated expression that makes Carmen blush— "that. Are you insinuating something?"

"*No.* Just shut up and keep walking," she snaps.

They head out of the building and walk over to the cafeteria. Usually, when she's with Jeroën, people make way for the two of them. Of course, with that came a lot of avoiding. Layla, Omar and Jeroën were the only people in her college who talked to her out of will.

"Come on," she says and leads him to an empty table. Earlier that day, Omar had sent her a text telling her that the two of them would come late.

Jeroën sits across her and she can feel his eyes on her. Suddenly, she feels self conscious. She tries to adjust her hair which is a total mess today and she straightens her yellow knee length dress.

"What is wrong?" he asks. "Why are you fidgeting?"

Carmen stops her feverish antics and coughs. "Um, because . . ."\

"Because?"

"Just because. Hey Jeroën," she says leaning in closer, "how do I look today?"

Jeroën stares at her incredulously. "Since when did you become so . . . unsure of yourself?"

"Just answer the question," she says rudely.

Jeroën crosses his arms and narrow his eyes. "I do not like it when humans are rude to *me*," he says pompously.

"Sorry," she mutters.

"And to answer your question," he says looking bored, "you look good."

"Really?" Carmen says with a million dollar smile. "Really?"

"What are you? A broken recorder?" he snorts. "Yes, you do. Do not act so surprised. You must hear that very often."

Carmen laughs without humour. "Ha, I don't."

"You do not?"

"I *don't*," she stresses. "Why do you talk so formally?"

"The last time I was sent down to Earth because of lack of interest was back in 1564. The fact that I am speaking like how I am right now is quite a miracle," he says with a proud smile.

Carmen claps weakly. "Yay."

"Hey, Carmen!"

Carmen whips her head around and sees Josh, one of the hotshot smart boys smiling at her. He's standing in front of two tables that are joined and tons of people are sitting there. He's in Carmen's English class and they hardly talked.

"Hey," she hollers back.

"Why don't you and your . . . friend come and sit over here?"

She could've said 'no'. She usually does. But having lived years of having the popular ignore her and that yearn to be among one of them filled her. So, she puts on a smile and says, "Sure!"

As she and Jeroën try to squeeze their way in two the two empty seat in the end of the table, she can hear disgusted sighs.

"*Ugh, why are they here?*"

"*God, he looks disgusting!*"

"*I can't sit next to him! He stinks!*"

"My grand mom's hair isn't as white as this guy's hair!'

So, when she sits down, she gives Jeroën's pale hand a reassuring squeeze. He looks at her like he's oblivious to all the whispering. He gives her a lopsided grin and looks at Josh who scowls at him.

"Carmen, how's college?"

Carmen resists the urge roll his eyes. "Huh, great, great."

"Yeah," says a brunette girl, "are you two like . . . dating or something?"

"No. We're not."

"Hey, Jeroën," says Josh. He looks like he's going to puke and Carmen instantly feels a sudden shot of disgust flush through her. No wonder, Iudex or whoever he was wanted all Deaths to come to Earth and see the darker side of the world.

Everyone sitting near him cranes their neck to see what he's going to say. "Where are you . . . from?"

"Some town near Sacramento."

"You have quite the accent, though."

"Yeah," Carmen says quickly. "He moved here when he was like 12."

Josh snickers. "I don't mean to be rude, Jeroën but you talk and look like my great grandfather."

"Yeah, what part of that wasn't offending?" Carmen scowls.

"William Xavier Junior? Is that your grandfather?" Jeroën says.

Josh looks mortified. "How do you know that, freak?"

"Hey—"

"Look, I don't know what you were thinking coming to this college. I don't even know how you survived high school with that disgusting face of yours," Josh says maliciously. "It's clear that you're an outcast and I don't like the fact that everyone's scared of you because you're fucking weird. You're one ugly faggot."

The cafeteria was filled with laughter and applauses as Carmen stands up in fury. She tries to shout at Josh but the hilarity in the cafeteria and the smirk on Josh's face drowns her anger. She clasps Jeroën's cold hand and tries to pull him up but he doesn't budge. Carmen looks down at him and freezes as he looks up at her.

His usually pale and impassive face is filled with pain and insecurity.

• • •

ADRIAN: *can't come now. Gotta drop Sheila.*

ADRIAN: *Go with Jeroën on a cab or somethin.*

"Okay?"

"Yeah," says Adrian, driving his car out of the parking lot. "Fasten that seatbelt."

"Where's Akelard?"

"Um, he's sick?" he lies. Akelard was completely against Adrian letting anyone other than Carmen and himself to know about the fact that he went for therapy.

"You know," hums Sheila, "I never picked you out to be a Nicholas Sparks fan."

"I don't know what you're talking about," Adrian says trying to be nonchalant.

"Sure," she drawls. She looks at Adrian with a small smile and she seems to be studying him.

"What?" Adrian asks, sneaking a look at her as he drives.

"Nothing much. You're just proving all the stereotypes wrong."

"Huh?"

"You're quite the Golden Boy. I'd expect you to be a player or some cocky ass who couldn't spell his name right" —Adrian's eyes narrow playfully— "but actually, you're a really decent guy who doesn't use people and throw them away."

"Ha, thanks."

"Why are you thanking me?" she chuckles. "Anyways, I like the fact that you're a sensitive guy deep inside."

"Yeah," he says slowly, "I'm pretty sensitive."

"See! You don't deny it like the other guys!"

"Yeah," Adrian says with a proud smile. "I still cry when a plant dies."

His shoulders feel like some huge rock's been taken away as he laughs along with Sheila.

• • •

Chapter 20

Adrian Sips His Fourth Cup of Coffee

"Should I remind you that it's the *twentieth century?*" he says exasperatedly. "Jeroën, can you try and act a bit . . . like a human?"

"Like extremely condemnatory and stuck up?" Jeroën snaps.

"Hey, I get that it was rude," says Adrian. "But you can't blame him."

It's Friday and Adrian has cancelled his plans to go out with Akelard because Carmen told him about what had happened and Adrian had promised himself that Jeroën was only leaving their apartment if he learned how to act like a human.

And yet, he can understand where Carmen's confusion's coming from. As far as he knew Jeroën, he never showed any signs of feelings . . . other than pride and hilarity.

Right now, Jeroën looked like a wounded puppy.

"First of all," says Carmen in a simpering sweet voice. "You have to stop saying 'cannot' and 'do not' and 'had not' and—"

"I get it," he says moodily. "I get it . . . fucker."

"Who taught you that?" Adrian scowls. "Trust me, that isn't the first step you take to act like a human."

"Chillax, bud . . . ?" Jeroën says, scrunching his nose. "These words sound bizarre."

"Well, what you say sounds weird too," says Carmen, folding her arms. "When someone offers you a hand as a greeting, you shake it. You don't stand there like a dummy," she snickers, remembering how he had acted when they had first met.

"But that is—"

"That's," Adrian and Carmen say in unison.

"Aye, that is just absurd."

"So are you," says Adrian ignoring Jeroën's glare. "I wish you would show the enthusiasm you showed when I taught you how to flirt."

"But that was interesting" whines Jeroën. "This is bloody confusing."

"You're impossible," she chuckles, shaking her head. "I'm going to study, now. Adrian, you can continue . . . teaching him."

• • •

She can smell happiness in the air.

As Carmen leans on the banister and places her hands on it so that she can keep herself steady, she looks down from her balcony and smiles softly as she takes in the jovial mood of the city.

City lights shine down on people who are full of life. She hears the laughter, the excited squeals of happiness and she sighs. She loves this.

"Nice . . . isn't it?"

She rolls her eyes, feeling amused. Carmen turns around and props her elbows on the banister as she quirks an amused eyebrow. "Hello stalker."

Jeroën looks at her flatly and says, "Shut up."

Carmen makes a motion of zipping her lips and throwing the key away. Jeroën strolls over to the banister and leans on it with a small smile playing on his lips.

"Seeing things like this makes me feel like there's good in this world disregarding all the stuck up arseholes and the dickheads—"

"Um, yeah," she giggles. "You've learned a lot from Adrian, I see."

Jeroën's eyes are thoughtful as he watches her giggle. Carmen sobers and says, "Isn't that the point, though? Aren't you supposed to be seeing and facing all the bad things in here so that you can be your . . . emotionless self?"

"Huh, yes. But I did meet you and . . . I feel good with you."

She blushes and coughs to clear the tension. "So, where's Adrian?"

"With Akelard."

"Okay." She feels awkward. It's amusing how the atmosphere changes with respect to how you feel about the person. Earlier, she never felt this congested and nervous around him.

"Are you alright?" He asks with a kind smile. Carmen feels something rumble in her stomach and she knows it's not hunger. It's something else.

"Peachy," she says and sighs as a whoosh of hair messes up her already messed up hair. She fusses with her hair for a few minutes.

"You know, I'll have to leave to Purgatory some time soon."

"Really?" she blurts. "When?"

Jeroën snickers at her expression. "I don't know. I'll get the message."

"One second." Carmen says apologetically, holding her hand up. "Do you feel hot? You can take off that jacket."

He sighs wearily and unzips his red leather jacket. As, he rolls the sleeves off his hands, Carmen tries to focus on his face and not on the swirling names appearing on his arms.

"Why do you wear jackets, anyways?"

Jeroën looks at her flatly. "Not everyone knows that I'm Death. Only you do so . . . the ideas of having people see names appearing and disappearing on my arms isn't pleasant, really."

"Oh yeah."

"That's the last thing I need."

"Ha, yeah."

Carmen lets out a loud sigh and clutches the cold railings feeling her hands tingle. She smiles and says, "I like this atmosphere. I really do."

"Me too," he says. "By the way, I forgot to ask. How was your time with your family?"

"Oh," she groans. "Eventful. I had *so* much fun."

"That's sarcasm, isn't it?"

"What would be the point of being sarcastic if I just gave away the fact that my statement was sarcastic?"

Jeroën narrows his grey eyes. "You're an ass."

"Pfft. You're no less," she smirks.

"You're an asshole."

"Asswipe."

"Fucker."

"Um . . . twat?"

"..."

Carmen smiles triumphantly. "You—"

"Imbecile!" he blurts.

She puts her hand over her mouth in mock mortification. "My, my. That's such a bad word! Who taught you that?"

Jeroën laughs loudly and says, "I really like your company, Carmen Collins."

"Well," she says trying to act nonchalant. "That feeling only goes one way."

"I'm not sure if that's a joke or what."

"..."

"*You suck!*"

• • •

Chapter 21

Carmen Scoffs in Disbelief

"You don't believe me?" Markus asks in a challenging voice.

"'Course I don't! You're a guy who's scared of butterflies—"

"Sh-h!" he hisses in annoyance. "I don't want the guys to hear that and so what? That doesn't mean I didn't go for skydiving."

"Remember that time Adrian and I dragged you with us when we went for sky diving? You cried your eyes out *and* you peed. It was like . . . the area was showered with your pee," she giggles.

"That was when we were sixteen," he snaps. "Anyways," he says hoarsely, leaning in closer. "I have to show you something."

He reaches out for something and she can hear shuffling of papers. Due to his frenzied movements, the camera goes black for a second or two until his beaming face appears again.

"What's it?"

He holds up a navy blue box and Carmen lets out a mortified gasp. He quickly says, "It's not a wedding ring, it's just a promise ring and—"

"Yes," Carmen says dramatically, fanning herself. "I promise you that I'll be with you forever!"

Markus gives her a flat look. She laughs and says, "You and Elle are that serious?"

"I love her," he says, "and she loves me."

"Then" —she moves her hand to make a sweeping gesture— "go forth, monsieur. You have my blessings."

"That's all I need," he says and smiles sincerely. "I wish I could see you right now."

"Me too, buddy," she says. "When are you going to Greece?"

"Next week," he yawns "I'll meet my there and she wants me meet Elle."

"Ouch," she says with sympathy as she recollects her time with the stout old woman. "I'll pray for her—oh hey!"

Jeroën smiles remotely and takes off his jacket and throws it on the couch. She's getting quite used to his arms.

"Is that Adrian?"

Carmen looks back at the screen and shakes her head. "Nope. Just another friend. Can I call you later?"

"You're ditching me for someone else?" he said in horror. "You—"

She shuts the laptop loudly only after feeling a tinge of annoyance at her behaviour. She usually hung upon him without any sort of explanation.

"Who's that?" Jeroën asks as he strolls over to the red bean bag that is across her and plops down on it.

"Markus. He's my friend—ex-boyfriend."

Jeroën's eyebrows rise up and he lets out a shrill whistle. "You had a boyfriend?"

"I'm just going to ignore the fact that you sound super surprised."

"And you actually keep in touch with him?" he chuckles. "Wow. That's something. Why did you two break up, if you don't mind me asking?"

Carmen leans back and crosses her right leg over her left. The evening's glow illuminates her den with a soft lighting and everything about the moment seems serene as she reminisces her time with Markus. "Um, we knew each other when we were twelve but you know, as we grew older" —she rolls her eyes— "*sparks* flew and so, when we turned fifteen, he asked me out."

"So, he cheated on you?"

"No! Where do you get these ideas from? Anyways, it was great. Markus' dad was a businessman and Markus was—or is— obsessed with travelling and whenever he would get back from his trips, he'd tell me about the place." A dreamy smile uplifts her face. "He had this talent . . . of painting the places with his words and I actually felt like I had been there with him. But," she sighs, shaking her head dramatically which cause Jeroën to chuckle softly, "as time passed, we felt more like friends. I mean, we spent more time talking about the places he had been compared to the time we made out. So, we broke up after a year but we've always been close."

"Ah," Jeroën says with a smile. "And is he dating someone else now?"

"Yup. Elle Colewood."

"Are you jealous?"

"Totally, Jeroën," she says flatly. "I'm planning to murder her the next time I see her. Markus is *mine*," she says in a deeper voice.

"Ugh. More work for me," he groans and they chuckle.

● ● ●

"Carmen, can you make it quick?" Akelard hollers.

"Yeah!" she yells back and sighs, picking up a red shirt from the pile of clothes that are strewn all over her bed. She plonks down on her bed and sighs jadedly.

"Why doesn't anything look good on me?" she groans running her bony fingers through her red hair. She can feel her insecurity clawing against her stomach. She gets up from her bed, clad in her thin camisole and underwear and walks to her vanity dresser. She peers at her reflection in the mirror and juts her lip out in displeasure.

Carmen taps her fingers on her flat stomach and pinches her sides, pulling on the skin. She scrutinises at her figure and suddenly, her body seems to be mocking her. Her waist gets smaller, her breasts become voluptuous and her emaciated face swells a little, giving more shape to her face.

"What the . . ." she gapes and blinks again and in a flash, the illusion is gone. All she can see now is her skinny figure. She lifts her fingers and she lets her fingers trace her lips that are reflected on the cold surface of the mirror.

"Why?" she whispers. "Why don't I look pretty?"

There's a knock on the door. "Carmen?"

She pulls at the ends of her red hair and the smell of her jasmine shampoo wafts by her nostrils. She pulls softly at first. She feels her insecurity slap her as she pulls her hair strongly. "Why?" she says loudly as tears roll down her face. "Why?"

Hastily, she rummages through her dresser. Makeup products that she hoped would make her look better falls from her frail grasp because she's sobbing and shivering. Carmen unscrews the cap of a foundation bottle and squirts a good amount of foundation on the back of her hand and she applies it on her face. Strangely, it seems like it's not enough because it doesn't covers up her freckles and so, she applies more.

She grabs a lipstick from the dresser and puts it on her lips.

Not enough.

She takes her mascara and brushes it through her long eyelashes.

Not enough.

Eyeliner, powder, eye shadows, and rouges found its place on her face and when she stared at the mirror, she saw her face with mixed colours.

She doesn't look beautiful.

"Ugh!" she screams and taking her hair dryer, she throws it on the mirror.

"CARMEN!"

She falls on the ground as the mirror breaks with a loud sound and as a few pieces prick her skin and fall to the ground, she sees her face in all the broken pieces of the mirror and she smiles weakly. Maybe that would make a difference.

But her smile, like the broken shards of the mirror, pierces her soul and mocks her.

Finally, the door's flung opens and Akelard barges in with a baseball bat in his hand. When he sees Carmen on the floor, half dressed and bleeding, he drops the bat, rushes towards her and pulls her to his chest ignoring the soft pricking of the mirror pieces on his chest.

"Oh. Carmen," he sighs. "What have you done?"

• • •

Chapter 22

Adrian Scowls at the Door

"You're acting like a child," Carmen says. "Just ring the bell."

"But," he yawns. "I want to go back and sleep! Why do we have to be here?"

"Just ring the bell, Adrian," Carmen says with a glare.

After a few more minutes of exchanging glares and profanity, Adrian steps on the doormat and rings the bell.

Carmen claps sarcastically. "I'm so proud of you, Adrian. So proud." She proceeds to wipe a fake tear from her eyes.

Akelard rolls his eyes at her. "Aren't they going to—?"

They hear the unlocking of a couple of locks and then the door is pulled open. Layla grins at them widely and steps aside, saying, "Come in!"

Omar and Layla's apartment, according to Adrian, had this strong smell of coffee and brownies which made his mouth water. The walls were painted a light orange and their den was scattered with textbooks and clothes.

"We thought you guys would come a bit late," Omar says, shutting the door after Akelard stumbles in. He locks the door and gestures to the den. "Sit down. We've got a couple of movies."

"Great," Carmen sighs, throwing herself on the red divan. "Bring it on."

• • •

"Adrian! Leave my hand right now," Omar demands as Adrian hides his head behind Omar's back.

"She's not going to die," Layla says flatly. She's been reciting this ever since they started watching the movie. "She's the heroine. If she dies, the movie ends."

"But—" he blubbers, letting go of Omar's arm. Omar immediately jumps off the cushion and hustles over to Carmen to sit next to her. "—her parents expect *so much* from her and now . . ."

Carmen starts to snicker. "Gee, Adrian. Grow up, would you?"

"Shut up."

Akelard, who shared the same sentiment as Adrian, wipes his teary face and croaks out, "I know, Adrian. I know."

Carmen bites her lip to stop the laughter from spilling laughter. "You know what? I heard some people talking about some club near Ostad hotel. How about we go there?"

"A club?" Akelard's face pales. "Um . . ."

"C'mon buddy," Omar says getting up. "Step out of your comfort zone."

• • •

"What *is* that?"

Adrian curls his lip in disapproval and nudges Akelard. "Drugs. Don't stare."

Akelard looks away quickly. He adjusts himself on the barstool and straightens his back. Carmen's snoring on the table, half drunk and Omar and Layla are dancing. "Why are they snorting it?" He asks, sneaking another look at the gang of intimidating looking men.

"Because they want to," he says curtly. "Don't be so fascinated."

"It looks kinda cool," he says with a shy smile. "It looks badass."

"How does snorting some kind of powder cool?" Adrian asks incredulously.

Akelard sticks his hand into the pockets of his khaki shorts and fishes out a packet of m&m's.

"Whatcha doin'?" He asks curiously.

He rips out the packet and puts out a few pebbles of m&m's. He places the heel of his palm on the pebbles and presses it hard with a screwed look on his face.

"What on—"

He retrieves his hand and dusts off the powder from his hands. He wipes off the coloured powder from the table and grins mischievously at Adrian.

"Dude," starts Adrian.

Akelard sniffs his cupped hand and snorts the powder.

"Oh my God!" Adrian croaks out as Akelard starts to sneeze. "Are you stupid?"

"I'm not responsible for my actions," he says drowsily, wiping his nose. "I'm drunk."

"So? You just snorted —"

He feels a tap on his shoulder. Slowly, he veers around and rases a questioning eyebrow at Layla who grins wildly at him.

"Don't be such a grandpa," she slurs, pulling his hand. "Come and dance."

After a lot of arguments and accusations of not acting like his age, Adrian, Akelard followed by a sleepy Carmen follow a bubbly Layla to the dance floor.

Aces & Spades was quite a famous club. As they danced in the midst of sweaty bodies with streaming lights showering on them, Adrian feels lighter. He doubts if it was the alcohol doing its job.

Carmen's shaking her hips and Omar's laughing at her drunken antics. Carmen grins and pulls Akelard towards her who's equally as drunk as her. He places his hands on her shoulder and they both squat down before jumping up.

Adrian has this strong urge to act like a stranger. Carmen gets herself another glass of vodka and resumes her ridiculous dance moves with Akelard.

The other day, when Adrian came back after having lunch with a friend, he found Carmen and Akelard with scratches all over their arms. They refused to talk about but when he saw small fragments of the mirror of Carmen's vanity dresser, he demanded to know. When he came to know about Carmen's sudden shot of low self esteem, he did not try to comfort her. He didn't want to seem hypocritical and give her stupid advice that he couldn't follow.

Carmen, Adrian and Akelard ate three buckets of chocolate ice cream on the terrace.

"Oh my God!"

He stirs out of his bubble and stares at a lanky woman in a cheetah dress staring at Carmen in livid anger.

"You just dropped your drink on my dress!" she screamed loudly. In a few seconds, they were the centre of attraction.

"No shit, Sherlock," giggles Carmen.

"Do you know who I am?" The lady glares at her. "I can make you pay for ruining this dress!"

"Uh. Listen ma'am," starts Omar.

"Apologise right now!" she yells.

Now, that was a simple task but Carmen was drunk. She rises up her hand and with a wicked smile, she holds up her middle finger.

She gapes and everyone in the club gasps in horror.

"How dare you?!"

"I'm so sorry!" Adrian rushes. "She's drunk and—"

He stops and his mouth goes dry when two strongly built men appear beside her and they look maliciously down at them.

• • •

"I want to stop!" pants Layla, slowing down. Omar looks back at her in horror and pulls her roughly. "You don't slow down!" he says. "You just keep running!"

"Why won't they stop?" Akelard gasps out of breath. "They're— shit, there's more!"

Adrian takes the risk of sneaking a look behind them and he gulps loudly as he finds a group of mean chasing them down the empty alley.

He sends Carmen a few curses in the process of pushing her forward. "This is like the mafia's chasing us!" she giggles hysterically. "So fun!"

He tries to yell some more curses but he's out of breath. They've been running for about half an hour now and they men seem to not give up.

"Hey! Look!"

Layla points at a parking lot that is crowded with bicycles. Judging by the maniacal grin on her face, he finds himself pulling out a cycle with much difficulty.

He's stealing a *bicycle*.

"I want the pink one," Layla whines, stamping the ground in annoyance.

"Just get one and come on! They're coming closer!"

With the wind beating against their faces and the rough paddling, Adrian feels like he has everything he needs. They're laughing their heads off, wheeling around stolen bicycles with no idea where they're going but that doesn't matter. Adrian feels like he has finally found his place in this world and he knows that the others have too.

And that's all that matters.

• • •

Chapter 23

Uncle Joe's Call Hits Her Like the Hangover in Her Head

"Adrian!" she yells, throwing the covers off her body. In a rush to get to the kitchen and start cooking, she falls on the cold floor.

"What?" Adrian yells back just as sleepily.

Muttering a string of colourful profanity, she pulls herself up and drags herself to Adrian's room.

"Get up!" she says pulling aside the curtains so that the sunlight can waken him up. It does.

"What the!"

"Get up. They're coming today!"

"Who is?"

"Our families!"

He sits up quickly, his eyes wide open. "Say what?"

She repeats herself and Adrian slaps his hand on his forehead. "Damn! I forgot that. What do we do?"

"Cook," she says flatly. "Chop, chop. Get to work, chef!"

"What about you?" he says, swinging his legs off the bed. "Laze around?"

"No," she says. She places her hand on her chest and with an offended frown; she dramatically chokes out, "How could you think of such a thing?"

"How could I not?" He mutters lowly.

• • •

He empties a bowl of zucchini pieces into the frying pan.

"You know," he says loudly over the hot sizzling sound of the frying pan and coughs, "dad's girlfriend? Clara? Apparently, dad doesn't want to tell me much about her."

"I heard," she groans, propping her elbow on the counter table. She had just finished cleaning the apartment. "Uncle Joe told me that she's an art therapist."

"Yeah?" he says absentmindedly, stirring the mixture of vegetables. "I just hope she's nice. Dad seems to *really* like her. Like *really really* like her."

"Uh huh."

As the oven dings, Adrian put on his kitchen gloves rushes over to it. He pulls open the door latch and pulls out a batch of cookies. He drops the tray of cookies on the kitchen table as it's hot. He hisses in pain and cradles his burnt hands to his chest.

"Smart move," Carmen snorts. She thrusts an ice bag to his chest and proceeds to devour a cookie.

"Hey," he frowns. "Don't finish 'em up."

"I won't." Her voice is muffled.

He opens his mouth to say something but he is stopped by the sudden ringing of his phone. Knowing who it is, he skips gleefully to the counter top.

"Lo?"

"Hey there, Adriana."

He ignores the second half of the greeting like he usually does. Hearing her voice—as cheesy as it sounded— always put a smile on his face.

"Sheila," he says breathily. Carmen's making some weird noise and starts to fan herself.

"Hey again," she chuckles. "So, what's up?"

"Uh, you know," he says hastily trying to cup Carmen's mouth that's making moaning noises. "Just . . . cooking. We have company for dinner."

"Uh huh. Who's it?"

"My dad, his girlfriend, Carmen's uncle and his wife," he says before fiercely mouthing '*stop that right now, Carmen!*'

"Well, I just called to see if you were free in the evening—"

"What for?"

"Slow down tiger," she laughs and Adrian's face instantly flushes a deep red. "I just wanted to see around. I thought you'd be free but it's okay."

"Damn, sorry Sheila. How 'bout tomorrow?"

"Err . . . nada. I'm meeting up Ram for some project."

"Oh . . . okay . . ."

"Yeah . . ."

". . ."

". . ."

"I have to go, then," she says quickly. "See you on Monday."

"Uh, okay. Bye," He sighs and hangs up the call.

"What's up?" Carmen asks softly as he lets out another distressed sighs.

"How much more obvious should I be to show her that I really like her?"

"Ad—"

"I mean I get that she's not human and shit but I really *do* like her." He closes the latch door of the oven loudly and shakes his head. "Forget it. There's no point in lamenting about things that won't happen. Have you set the table yet?"

•••

"Did you—holy shit, you *did!*" Adrian gawks at his father who tries to give him a glare.

"Shut up," he hisses after giving his girlfriend a sweet smile.

"You dyed your hair," Adrian says with an amazed look. "I thought you hated people who dyed their hair!"

"I did? Oh well."

"Dad, you're doing this for *her?*"

Steven's sunken cheeks flush red and he ducks his head in embarrassment as his son starts to laugh.

"What's up?" Uncle Joe asks. They are seated in the lounge, sipping their steaming mugs of hot chocolate. The ladies are in the kitchen; gossiping and helping Clara prepare her famous dish — apple crumble.

"Dad's going all out for Clara," Adrian snickers.

"You'll go all out too when you find someone you love," said Uncle Joe in a deep tone. "Speaking of which, is there a girl?"

"Nope."

"Really?"

"Yup."

• • •

The wind whispers into his ear and his eyes sting a little.

Her photograph looks like a relic of tears and sleepless nights. She's smiling back at him, her smile so elegant and peaceful which is in contrast to the storm raging in his heart.

"She's . . ." he swallows thickly, "pretty nice. Dad seems to really like her. She's funny and . . . smart and dad's really happy with her but he's not himself around her. Dad apparently likes Guy Williams," he snorts. "Remember how he used to shove cottons into his ears when you played his songs? Carmen told me that it'll change."

He runs his sweaty palm on his blue shorts and sniffs. He can hear Carmen's clear laugh and Akelard's contagious one which makes him chuckle a bit.

"The people here are nice," he says with a sad smile. "I mean, I'm not so close to them compared to how I am with Carmen but they're great. You'll love them. In fact, you should meet Layla. She's an exact replica of you when it comes to cooking." He bites his lip in embarrassment and continues, "When she cooked *Empanadas* and *Patatas Bravas* . . . I almost cried, I did. It tasted exactly like yours and I just . . . wish you were here," he whispers the last bit like it's a secret. "I just wish you were here."

• • •

Chapter 24

Adrian's Eyes Skim Through the Calendar

His face pales when he sees the date. He scrambles off his bed and rushes to the calendar that's hung above his study.

26th February

CARMEN'S FAM

"Twenty sixth," he whispers, "that's tomorrow."

And he wonders if she remembers. In the midst of college and friends, he wouldn't blame her if she forgot about it. He rubs his sleepy eyes wearily and ruses to the bathroom to wash himself up.

• • •

His mother used to serve him a soup of cold soup whenever she had something serious to say.

The last time she served it to him was a week before she died. Adrian remembers the scene bitterly how his mother informed him that his dad lost his job and they would have to limit their expenses.

So, he pushes a bowl of cold soup towards Carmen whose eyes are glued on her phone screen. She chuckles at something and shakes her head.

"Uh, Carmen?"

"Huh? Oh yeah," she says placing the phone on the table. She gives him a smile and takes a spoonful of his soup. "Mmm, tastes great."

He clears his throat and says, "Carmen, do you know what today's date is?"

"Nope. All I know is that it's a Friday," she smiles cheekily. "What's up?"

"Tomorrow's the twenty sixth, Cars."

Her face pales instantly. She drops the spoon and it drops on the bowl laden with soup.

"T—tomo—"

"Tomorrow," he says.

"Oh no," she says hoarsely. "I actually forgot. I *actually* forgot."

"Carm—"

"How could I forget?" she says slapping her forehead. "How on earth?"

"It's okay," he says softly, "it's okay, really."

"It's not okay!" she says fiercely. "I just forgot about them! How the hell . . . I never forgot 'bout it no matter what happened" —here she runs her fingers through her red hair— "I just . . . dad would've been so disappointed in me."

• • •

"What's wrong?"

"Nothing," she replied tautly.

"Obviously something's wrong otherwise you wouldn't be so—"

"Just leave me alone!"

Omar's brown eyes widen at her snarky tone and he nods briskly before storming out of the lecture theatre. She huffs loudly and buries her head in her hands that are folded in front of her not feeling a tinge of contrition.

She remembers how she used to be back at home. A week before her dad's and brother's death anniversary, she would write poems and pluck out flowers—daffodils to be exact from Aunt Lucy's garden discreetly. She remembers how Uncle Joe told her that if she buried her poems to them in between her brother's and father's grave, when the paper would dissolve into nothing—just like them, it would go up and her father would read it out to her brother and like the old days, they would tease her silly handwriting and praise her at the same time.

When she grew older, she still continued to do it. She would write poems and bury them in the ground but now, all she had was regret.

After an hour of brooding in resentment and glaring at the white board, she feels a presence beside her. Knowing who it is, she shifts slights so that her body's facing the opposite wall.

"Carmen?"

". . ."

"Carmen?"

"Go away, Jeroën."

"Layla told me that you were pissed off for something. What's up?"

"Nothing," she groans loudly. She clenches her eyes shut as she hears him plop down next to her.

"No something's wrong and you—"

"*Nothing's wrong!*" she yells loudly. All that anger that she had felt about the negligence toward her family's death was flushing out of her and she could feel her voice echo through the empty lecture theatre.

But Jeroën remained unfazed. He blinks twice, unemotional and just shrugs. "What's wrong?"

• • •

"I feel like I'm disrespecting them by not remembering it," she finishes with a grave sigh. She shakes her head and a few strands slip from behind her ear and she tucks it back in.

"Ah, I see," he hums leaning back in his chair.

"I'm glad you do."

Jeroën lets out a chuckle and says amicably, "What? You don't like that I do?"

"I just expected something . . . wiser?"

"You think I'm wise?" he asks with a strange gleam in his eyes. "You do?"

She rolls her eyes. "Whatever."

"Maybe you should take your own advice."

"What's that supposed to mean?"

"Remember how you used to tell me how you hate regretting over things?"

". . . Yeah?"

"Well, I think you should really follow your advice," he says with a small shrug. "If it helps. I swear your life would be so much better."

"Oh."

She looks at him and when her blue eyes collide with his piercing grey ones, she realises that there's one thing she's certain about.

That she is irrevocably in love with Jeroën Jarvis.

• • •

Chapter 25

Carmen Stirs Slowly and Groans Loudly

"Carmen?" he says nudging her. She wakes up with a groan and rubs her eyes wearily. She looks out of the window and when she sees the surroundings, she heaves a long sighs and says, "Are you coming?"

He shakes his head. It's almost like a routine now. Whenever he dropped her off to the graveyard, she would always ask him *"are you coming?"* and he's always shake his head a no.

He hasn't visited her grave since the funeral. He would never accompany his dad to the graveyard. He could never watch his dad place his mom's favourite flowers on her grave —white roses and he could never watch his dad break down.

Adrian doesn't quite know how to decipher the feelings that crawls all over his body whenever he nears any graveyard. He doesn't know if it's fear or hatred. All he knows is that he's never stepped foot since eight years.

And he doubts if he ever will.

• • •

The graves are covered with wisterias and dirt.

It looks the same like it did last year and yet it doesn't. She observes that the graves look older but it still has that same ambience. She drops to her knees and she doesn't bother if her jeans get dirty.

She places the jasmines on her dad's grave and roses on her brother's grave. She sits down on the edge of her father's grave and a large blue wisteria that is strewn over the headstone reminds her of her father's eyes—identical to hers.

So, she starts to talk. She tells him about college, the people she met and the places she's been to. She tells him about Jeroën (albeit a bit quietly) and she tells him how the friends that she has made don't made her feel like a Fearless Freak.

And she could feel her dad bobbing his head up and down to the point where his glasses would slide off his nose. She could feels him muttering those absentminded 'oh's and she could feel him give her those flat looks when she got off topic and she could feel him ruffle her red hair in amusement.

The trees start to whisper as the winds grows stronger and goose bumps unravel her skin, she suddenly feels the deep longing for her father to be next to her.

• • •

Carmen eyes Adrian pensively. She clears her throat and as Adrian starts the engine, she places her hand on his hand which rests on the gear.

"Adrian, come on. Just go for once."

"No. Buckle up, would you?"

"Adrian just—"

"I said I don't want to go!" he yells loudly and pulls off his hand. But that doesn't startle Carmen. She's used to this.

"You've never been there and it's really—"

"Oh so *now* you have a problem with that?" he fumes. He give out a humourless laugh and says, "*Now* you have a problem with that, huh?"

"No, I don't and you know that but—"

"Could've fooled me," he mutters. "Just put on your seatbelt."

"Would you *stop*? Can you just listen to me for once? You haven't gone there for years and you're keeping all this guilt buried within you for years. Just go there and . . ." she sighs and in a softer tone, she continues, "you'll feel much better, I promise."

"You don't understand, okay? It's not that I don't want to go, it's that I *can't*. I can't face her at all."

That doesn't word on Carmen. Her blue eyes don't flicker in submission. Instead, they stare back at him without an ounce of sympathy.

"Just go."

• • •

His feet crunches up the dead leaves as he nears her grave.

Adrian spots a bouquet of white roses placed neatly on the gace. He squats down and pinches the bridge of his nose.

And like the tears that are running down his face, the words and feelings that he kept buried all along began to flow out.

He tried to slow down the pac because he was blabbering now. *I'm sorry, mom, i really am. I'm just too scared . . . and i feel guilty and I'm sorry I acted like a coward, I really am. I'm not like you and I'm so sorry.*

Gradually, his tears dried up and instead of apologising, he started telling her of his friends and of Sheila. He told her about Jeroën and he could imagine her quirking a dubious eyebrow like she always used to whenever Adrian told anything absurd to her.

(Which was every time.)

He tells her of his nightmares and he tells her how much he misses her. He tells her that he feels like the only one who's frozen in this oblivion that disables him to look around and think about the others.

In the end, he bends his head down in prayer, his hands crossed and his lips moving wordlessly.

When he stands up and dusts off his pants, he feels like he's also dusting away the bundle of burden he carried with him all along. He feels considerably lighter and wonders why he never did it all along.

• • •

Chapter 26

Adrian's Got Birds Tweeting in His Head

He's bobbing his head to some classic song and he feels great. He feels like he can *finally* say that he's happy and this time, it is the truth.

"Are you on drugs or something?" Akelard asks dubiously as Adrian proceeds to do a few dance moves.

"You mean did I snort on m&m's?" Adrian retorted.

"..."

"Kidding," he chuckles. "I just feel really happy today."

"I can see that," he mutters. "On another note, I have to . . . tell you something."

"Shoot, brother from another mother."

"..."

"Okay *fine.* Tell me."

"You know that cafe we go to? Für Elise?"

Adrian nods jovially. Akelard screws his eyebrows together and looks at him which resulted in tripping on someone.

"S—sorry," he stammers, his hands shivering as a girl with red hair bends down to pick up her binders.

"S'okay," she says smiling.

After she walks by, Adrian ruffles his black hair and says, "Not everyone's a bad guy, okay? So yeah, tell me. What about that cafe?"

"Well," he mutters shyly, "there's this one guy—"

"And you like him?"

"P—pretty much."

Adrian's pensive mood scares him a bit. His lips are pursed and he doesn't say anything.

"What's wrong?"

Adrian stops walking and looks at Akelard, his green eyes looking lighter in the sunlight. "I like you, Akelard."

Akelard's eyes widen in shock and he drops his books in shock. His hands start to shiver and he stammers out, "w—what?!" Adrian reaches forward quickly as Akelard's legs give out beneath him. He's steadied by Adrian who catches his elbows and pulls him up.

"Gee, I didn't know you couldn't take a joke. I was just kidding. I'm as straight as . . . a ruler."

"That's a—a horrible an—analogy and don't say things like that!" He scowls. "It's not funny."

"Sorry," Adrian says holding his hands up in resignation. "Continue, would you?"

"Fine," he grumbles, rubbing his sweaty palms on his khaki pants. "He's gay too and I *really* like him."

"I want to meet this guy," he says firmly. "You make him sound like he's some kind of God. Obviously," he scoffs, "he can't be hotter than me."

"Sure," Akelard rolls his eyes. "Anything that makes you sleep at night."

After bunking the first lecture, Adrian decides he would attend the next one as Sheila would be there. He spots her leaning against the wall, sitting on a seat at the corner of the class.

He walks up to her sits next to her. She doesn't notice his presence. Instead, she draws a few doodles on her notebook. Her blonde hair is pulled up in a high ponytail and her reading glasses almost slide off her long nose. She pushes it back up and as Adrian clears his throat to get her attention, she looks at him startled and relaxes.

"Oh hey," she says. "How're you?

"Great!" he chirps happily. "How about yourself?"

"Yeah? I'm . . . fine? What's up with you?"

He leans in closer and says, "Yesterday I went to see mum."

She furrows her eyebrows and frowns, "I thought . . . oh! Okay! I took that literally," she says sheepishly. "I'm so proud of you though. Is that why you're really happy now?"

"Yup," he smiles widely. "I feel great!"

"You should've done this before, huh? It's nice to see you smile freely."

Her brown eyes, magnified by the thick reading glasses that she wore, meet his green ones shyly and they smile in unison.

• • •

"Why . . . are there two pairs of shoes in front of your door . . . ?"

Akelard's black eyes widen in shock as he takes in the sight before him. A pair of expensive pink shoes and a pair of brown leather shoes were lined up neatly on the mat before the door. He whispers hoarsely, "They're here."

Adrian cocks an eyebrow. "Say what?"

Akelard's hands start to shiver and his lower lips quivers in fear. He wipes his sweaty palm on his polka dotted blue shorts. He tries to bite his lip but he's shivering too much.

"Hey, buddy," Adrian says worrisomely. "Dude, we'll just see who the intruders are and—"

The door opens and a couple grins widely at the three friends.

• • •

Her lips are blood red.

Even though she had the sweetest smile Adrian had ever seen, he could not help but be spiteful.

Akelard's parents looked expensive. His mom looked like him with the black hair and black eyes and pale skin. She had a simpering smile playing on her lips and her fingers that were decorated by diamond rings were crossed on her lap neatly.

"And you are Akelard's friends?" she asks.

Carmen and Adrian nod mutely.

Akelard's dad coughs to clear the awkwardness but it increases the tension of the room. He's wearing an expensive grey suit and his white French beard and bald head makes him look really intimidating.

"That's so nice!" she gushes and her red lips widen into a grin. Evil, Adrian thinks. She's the witch herself. "Akelard always had difficulty in making friends and I'm *so* glad that he's changed now."

"Are you?" Adrian retorts tautly before he can stop himself but he doesn't feel regret wash over him. Instead, he feels satisfaction.

A look of disbelief plasters itself on her face. She lets out a nervous laugh and dabs her forehead with her handkerchief. "Of course I do. I'm his mother."

Adrian clenches his teeth to stop himself from insulting her.

Akelard's father turns to Akelard and Adrian hates how Akelard's body recoils back in fear. He doesn't like how Akelard's body is pressing back into the couch and he doesn't like the way he's gulping.

"And how are you?" he asks.

"F—fine."

He rolls his eyes and says, "You still stutter?"

"I—I—I— tr—tried—"

"Yeah, he does," Carmen cuts in. She leans forward and his eyebrows shoot up at her bold posture. "But of course, you'd know that. You are, after all, his father."

"Uh—"

"So," claps Akelard's mother. "How did you guy meet?"

"We're his neighbours," says Adrian in a bored tone. "And I'm in his college."

At this, she throws a scowl at him. He feels a flare of notorious pride when he sees her curl her lip in distaste at his curt answers.

"So, Akelard. We came here for a reason," says Akelard's dad and he raises his eyebrows at Adrian and Carmen who stare back flatly at him.

"Uh, it's kinda private."

They don't move an inch.

He tightens his jaw and his steely grey eyes glare at Akelard, questioning him on his choice of friends. *"Akelard, Du musst kommen nach hause."*

Akelard widens his eyes and his legs start to shake. "No. N—no. *Ich-ich Wnt, hier zu bleiben. Ich werde s-studie und werde einen Anwalt.*

"Halt den Mund! Du zurück nach Hause! Sie haben ein zu kümmern!"

Adrian's looking back and forth. He's trying to understand the situation. He silently curses himself for failing German back in High School.

"I—please . . . I'm happy here and—I . . ." Akelard's weeping now. He's blubbering sloppy words and his shoulders are convulsing. Akelard's dad rolls his eyes and his mom shakes her head.

"Ugh, Akelard, stop crying for Christ's sake and fucking grow up! *Wer weint jetzt?"* She lets out a shrill high pitched laugh. *"Habien Sie noch in Ihen Hose pissen."*

"Genug! Es ist mir egal, ob du seine Mama oder Papa aber Sie nicht, ihn so reden Wagen!"

Everyone stills and slowly veers their eyes to Carmen who's breathing heavily. Her tall figure is looming over Akelard's mom who's staring at the long finger Carmen's pointing at her.

"You two are pathetic excuses of parents! You just randomly pop out of nowhere and tell him to come back? Do you even know him? You guys just rejected him because he wasn't 'worthy enough' to be in your family! You think this is some kind of switch? You call him when you want to and you tell him to go when you want to?"

"Excuse—"

"I'm not done," she snarls. "I'm not done, you get it? Akelard's a great guy and he doesn't deserve this. He doesn't deserve to be shunned because he isn't like how you want him to be. He has dreams too! He wants to be a lawyer and now, here you are, ordering him to come back and work in your company. Can you hear yourself?"

Akelard's mother's shivering just like her son but unlike him she's not shivering in fear. She's shivering in anger.

"You will *not* talk to my husband like that. You clearly don't know who we are to go around blurting bullshit like that and you clearly don't know anything about my son to keep—"

"To keep what?" Carmen demands, inching closer. "I know more about your son than you do and you know why? Because I *talk* to him. Because I love him for whom he is. I'm not disgraced by his presence. I don't find the fact that he's gay disgusting. I don't find the fact that he pees whenever he gets really anxious or scared repulsive."

"And you know what that means?" Adrian says as he gets on his feet. He has a small smirk on his face and he opens the door. "That means you have absolutely nothing to do here."

• • •

"So, like, I know that it feels really awkward and shit but you know what always helps?"

"W—what?"

"Food."

"Great idea. You're paying."

"I'm not buying. I'm *making*."

". . ."

". . ."

"How 'bout some pasta, eh?"

"Yeah. No."

"I—I'm just go—going to go there."

"You guys suck. Period. And you know what else?"

"What?"

"My birthday's next week. Of course, Cars. *You* knew that."

"Uh . . ."

"What! Akelard, c'mon man."

"Um, well, y'know . . ."

"I've said it before and I'll say it again: You guys suck."

• • •

Chapter 27

Carmen Unlocks the Door With a Huff

As soon as the door opens, she flings herself inside and dumps her books on a couch. She rummages her fingers through her knotted hair and rubs her cramped neck.

"Hate you, Adrian," she groans. Sweat trickles down her back and she shifts uncomfortably.

"I'm sorry," he says, "but I *had* to study! My exams are next week."

She swivels around and glares at Adrian who locks the door. "You couldn't spare like . . . ten minutes to pick me up? I had to *walk* back home!"

"You could've taken a cab or something," he says defensively. His hair's dishevelled and he has dark circles under his eyes.

"I forgot my purse," she mumbles.

"And whose fault is that?"

"And why is it so hot in here?" she gasps out and wipes off the sweat forming on her forehead. "Is the air conditioner broken or something?"

"Yup. I've been trying to fix it but I couldn't do it by myself. Help me out?"

• • •

"Fuck it!"

"Hey, don't throw that—you dumbass! I almost did it!"

"You 'almost did' it for like two hours. Come on; let's go to Akelard's apartment."

"Nope. I'm going to fix this."

"..."

"..."

"..."

"..."

"..."

"Okay. Fine."

So, after a few minutes of bickering back and forth, the dup make their way across to Akelard's apartment. Much to Akelard's amusement, they entered his apartment begrudgingly.

"What's up?"

"He ruined the air conditioner."

"I did not. It—"

"Yada, yada, yada."

"Come here you—"

• • •

She scribbles the equation with a huff.

Scratching her scalp with the end of her pencil, Carmen sticks out her tongue and screws her eyebrows together in confusion as she tries to solve a problem. He writes out an alternative answer, muttering curses under her breath only to cut it out later.

"Ugh!" she groans, leaning back in the chair, rubbing the crease that's forming between her eyebrows. "I hate you, Maths."

There's a knock at the door and Carmen mutters a soft 'yes'. The door is pushed open and Akelard stares at her with wide eyes.

"What's up?"

"He—he's here!"

"Who?"

"H—Him."

Carmen rolls her eyes and sighs. "And who does 'him' refer to?"

"Je—Jeroën!"

At this, Carmen grins widely. "He is? How did he know that I was at your apartment?"

"I—I don't know. Just get him out of here!"

"Why? What's wrong?"

"He's weird and creepy and weird and he just looks so intimidating and—"

"Hey?"

Akelard let out a small yelp and clutches the door knob as Jeroën appears behind him. He has a lazy smirk drawled on his face as he takes in Akelard's feverish antics.

"Akelard, go and watch TV with Adrian if you're that scared."

He scurries away.

Jeroën chuckles and shuts the door behind up. Carmen smiles at him

"What are you studying?"

"Maths. Which explains this," she says pointing at her mess of red hair.

"It's pretty easy, actually."

She snorts and says, "You don't even study. You just get good marks because you're Death."

"I—"

"—prefer Jeroën. Sorry, it just came out."

Jeroën shrugs and sits on Akelard's bed. He leans back on the headboard and trails his fingers on the red satin bed covers. Carmen watches him with a small smile before shaking her head and resuming with her calculations.

After suppressing her urge to tear her book into pieces and burn it, she swivels around in her chair and looking at Jeroën who's busy reading some magazine, she asks, "Hey . . . could you . . . um . . ."

Jeroën looks up from the magazine with a smug smile. "Could I what? Come on, it's not that hard."

"Could you . . . help me out?"

Jeroën laughs and says, "You sound like you're choking."

". . ."

"Fine."

He throws his legs off the bed and hops over to Carmen. She bites her lip as Jeroën hovers over her. His lips are moving but Carmen can't hear a thing. She's just staring at his grey eyes.

"Is there something on my face?"

Carmen blinks and smiles sheepishly and says, "W—what no! I was listening to you."

He looks at her flatly. "Right."

She smiles hesitantly and clears her throat. "Uh . . . you were saying?"

"Yes. As I was saying—"

". . . wa—hey . . . ?"

Jeroën straightens himself in a second and Carmen's cheeks are flushed red as she sees Adrian's teasing grin.

"Sorry for interrupting you guys," wink, wink, "but I just wanted to say that Akelard and I were going out for a jog."

". . . okay."

". . ."

"You can, um, continue with whatever you guys were doing." With that said, he gives Carmen a wink before slamming the door.

"He's a weird guy."

Carmen laughs nervously, mentally making plans on how to execute Adrian's murder. "That he is."

• • •

"He's a very choosy guy," mutters Carmen rubbing her chin. "Last year I knitted him this blanket that was filled with his favourite superheroes. He liked that a lot but I don't know what to get him now."

"I don't know either," Jeroën says with a shrug. "But I know that he likes Nicholas Sparks. So, I got him a few DVD's of the movies and a few books."

"He'll love it," she says and squints at the shelf of records again. "Should I get it for him or what?"

"Make it quick, would you? These people are making me shifty," he says uncomfortably. He pulls the hood tautly so that no part of his face could be seen. People were looking at him and Carmen nodded. "Okay, c'mon, let's go."

•••

Chapter 28

Adrian Opens His Eyes in Fright

"Happy birthday!"

"What the actual . . ." he trails as he lifts his head to take in Carmen on him before plopping back on bed. "Oh yeah!"

"Don't tell me you actually forgot it," she scoffs getting off him. "You kept screaming it into my ear yesterday."

He sits up and grins widely, rubbing away the crust in the corner of his eyes. "Man, I'm actually nineteen!"

Carmen smiles. "That you are. Here," she says, pulling out his gift from behind her back, "that's your gift. I'm sorry if it sucks."

"I'll never forgive you," he says darkly before smirking at her scowl.

He tries to be gentle at first because Carmen's wrapping of gifts is so beautiful that he didn't want to unwrap it. He gingerly pulls the ribbon and pulls out the tape. After spending too much time on fiddling with the other ribbons, he ends up tearing the whole packaging.

"Oh. My. God."

"Do you like it?" she asks, biting her lip. "I wasn't too sure . . ."

"*This is awesome!*" he yells as he takes out his vinyl and records. "Oh my God. Bob Marley, Elvis Presley, The Beatles, Pink Floyd—Carmen, God, this is awesome!"

"Whew," she sighs. "I thought you wouldn't like it."

"I love it," he whispers, his eyes skimming through the records. "I love it."

"Well, hurry up then. You have college don't you?"

"Yeah," he groans. "Why do you have a holiday today?"

She shrugs. "Dunno, don't care. Get going!"

He quickly takes a shower and gets dressed. Unlike most days when he throws on a plain shirt, today on account of his birthdays, he put on a white shirt, black dress pants and a red tie. Having finished his morning routine, he hurries to the kitchen and has his usual glass of orange juice. After being pushed out by Carmen, he knocks on Akelard's door.

"Oh, good morning and happy birthday," Akelard smiles as he locks the door behind him.

Adrian blinks and grins. "Thanks! I can finally boss you around because I'm older than you."

"That never stopped you," he mutters and instantly dodges Adrian's nudge.

• • •

"Why . . . are you smiling like you won million dollars?"

Adrian smiles widely as Sheila eyes him like he sprouted an extra head. "You don't know?"

"Don't know what?"

"Why I'm smiling?"

"No, dummy," she says, rolling her eyes. "That's why I asked you. And why are you dressed so . . . formally?"

"Because it's my birthday today!" he says excitedly and when the whole library glares at him, he clears his throat and straightens his tie as his cheeks turn red.

"It's your birthday today?"

"That's what I said."

Sheila purses her red lips and says, "Why didn't you tell me before?"

"Um . . . I don't know but who cares? Do you want to come over and—"

"You don't care but I do!" she says, interrupting him. "Now that I think of it, I'm standing like an idiot right next you while everyone else are wishing you!"

"Sheila . . ." Adrian says slowly. "It's okay, really. I'm not that big on birthdays."

". . ."

"Okay, so maybe I am but it's *fine* really."

She rolls her eyes and releases a huff. "Happy birthday, you ass." And with that being said, she gives him a glare and speeds down the hallway.

"What's up with her?"

• • •

"This is great."

"It really is," Carmen says, her voice muffled with potato fries. "I love this hotel."

"You guys should thank me," Omar says with a pompous smile.

"Still has a weird ass name. Why would anyone name a hotel *Flankton?*" says Layla with a shrug. She sips her drink.

"Well," Omar sighs. "Now it's gift time." He reaches down for a pink box wrapped with white frills which makes Adrian roll his eyes. Omar narrows his eyes at him and says, "Don't judge."

"I didn't even say anything."

"I saw the way you looked at the gift."

"Just give it to me."

Omar gives it to him with a dramatic huff earning chuckles from his friends. Adrian tears off the packaging with wide eyes glistening with excitement.

"Hey!" Adrian beams. "You got me the game I wanted."

"That's the point of having birthdays, man."

"And . . . you got me a twenty dollar gift card to Starbucks."

"Yup."

"The originality and uniqueness in this gift is making me cry."

"Is that sarcasm?"

"Well," Layla interrupts. "I'm sure that you'll like my gift even more."

She hands him a square shaped box with brown packaging which Adrian rips off in no time. He holds up two books and a folded shirt with a wide smile.

"You got me two Nicholas Sparks' books!"

"I did!"

"And you got me the limited edition shirt that I wanted!"

"I did!"

"I love you, Lay!"

"Uh . . ."

"As a friend, dummy."

• • •

"Are you kidding me right now?" Adrian asks flatly.

"What is it?" Carmen asks looking up from her magazine.

"'When Carmen gave me your *Brunswick stew,* I thought it would be great because it looked freaking great! I swear to God, Adrian. I almost died. So, this book will teach what to cook and *how* to fucking cook it. Much love, Markus.' He got me 'Cooking for Dummies'!"

Carmen laughs. "Not that bad, eh? At least now you'll know how to cook. What did Uncle Joe get you?"

Adrian grabs a red box and rips off the ribbon. He opens the flap of the box and cocks an eyebrow as he looks down. "He got me a pair of dumbbells."

". . . okay. Is there a note or something?"

"No? Well, I did think about joining the gym so, I guess this is cool?" Adrian shakes his head and lets out a chuckle. "Uncle Joe always gives out weird gifts."

He picks up the last package and smiles softly. His dad's gifts were the best. He opens the flaps of the box and takes out the paper balls. He takes out a frame that held a picture of his mom and him with ice cream on the noses, giggling.

For memories we wish to revive again. Happy birthday, son.

He sets down the picture gently and takes out another box. He furrows his eyebrows and tears out the packaging.

"Aw man, he got me a Rolex!"

"Great."

"You jealous, eh?"

"*Sure.* I'm burning with jealousy."

Adrian chuckles and says, "Where's Akelard?"

"In your room," she says brushing back her red hair. "He said he was setting up something."

"Oh God," he sighs and rushes to his room to find it closed. He knocks on his auburn coloured door and asks, "Akelard, you in there?"

"Yeah!" *Thump.* "Wait a second!" *Thump.* "Okay, come in!"

Adrian opens the door slowly preparing himself for Akelard to do some stupid ninja move on him but instead he was welcomed by complete darkness.

"Hey buddy, you in there?" Adrian asks warily.

He steps in and shuts the door behind him. He reaches for the switch but is stopped when all of a sudden; the room is engulfed in small spots of white light.

"Here," he hears Akelard's breathy whisper. "This is my gift to you. A star projector. It's pretty lame but . . . um, I know how much you love them. So, this is for those starless nights, man."

"Wow," he whispers as the stars keep twinkling at him. His eyes are watery and he can't help but gape in wonder. "Wow."

"I'm guessing you like it?"

"I fucking love it," he breathes. He touches a small spot of light and lets out a breathy laugh. "Thank you."

"You're welcome."

"No seriously. Thank you."

"Yeah, I know. You're welcome."

"Thank you."

"I got it the first time. You're welcome."

". . ."

". . ."

". . ."

"No—"

"Thank you."

•••

Chapter 29

Carmen's Eyes Glisten in the Sunlight

"Don't you feel awkward?" she asks Jeroën as he pulls his legs up to h is face. "You're the only one fully clothed here."

"Yeah, well. They don't have names appearing and disappearing on your hands."

"Ha-ha, they'd think it's some new type of invention of having tattoos go and come."

Jeroën lets a small smile crack his impassive face and he grabs a fistful of sand before letting it slip through his fingers.

"Before," Carmen says. "Adrian and I would love going to the beach at night so we would sneak out and go to the beach."

"And do what?"

"Nothing really. Sometimes, we'd go for a swim. Sometimes, we'd build sandcastles and stamp on them. Most of the times, we would talk."

"You would talk? For hours?" Jeroën gives her a small smile. "About what?"

"Things that wouldn't interest you at all," she says with a wink. "Hey Jeroën?"

"Yeah?"

Carmen straightens the creases of her floral dress. Jeroën complimented the way she looked in floral dresses at least ten times. Carmen felt like she could shed away her insecurities around him.

"Tell me the weirdest experience you've had."

"Uh . . . I never had one?"

"Come on buddy. I'm trying to make a conversation out here."

Jeroën laughs and Carmen instantly feels like she accomplished a task. "Um . . . well, I've never had any weird experiences to be honest. Death isn't a joke."

She cringes. "Yeah. It isn't."

"But there's something I have to tell you."

"What's it?"

"I'll . . . have to leave some time soon."

"Why? It's just twelve in the afternoon."

"No," he says rolling his eyes. "I have to go go."

Carmen juts her lip in confusion. "I'm not really catching the drift."

He sighs wearily. "Carmen, who am I?"

"Uh . . . Jeroën?"

"No! Who am I really?"

"Death?"

"Yes. And what's my job?"

"To kill—"

Jeroën clears his throat with a flat look.

"Of course," she says rolling her eyes. "You *take* away people's souls. How could I forget?"

"Yeah, I'll have to get back to that job."

Carmen stares at him in shock. She blinks a few times and says, "Did you just say what I think you said?"

"Well, did you hear something along the lines of me leaving?"

"Yeah?"

"That's exactly what I said."

"Wait—you're leaving? Like you're actually leaving?"

"Sometime soon, yes. I've spent too much time here."

"So . . . you're going to Purgatory?"

"Yes."

"But you can't go," she whispers softly, her mind racing through different thoughts. "You can't go because . . ."

"Because?"

"Because . . ." Her throat feels dry and she feels like the words are slipping from her mouth.

"Carmen?" He asks softly, leaning closer. "What's wrong?"

Carmen clears her throat trying to collect herself. "How can you leave? Life's must better here."

"Life?" He chuckles shaking his head. His grey eyes appear very light in the sunlight. "You're talking to *me* about life?"

"I—I mean," she stammers. "You can't just *leave!*"

"Why not?"

"Because I love you!"

In the back of her head, Carmen can actually feel the throb of her heart and it's making her head pound.

"... *what?*"

Carmen meekly looks up at him and he's staring at her with wide eyes. His usually pale face is even paler. She tucks a strand of her red hair behind her ears and sinks her toes in the sand, desperately trying to not meet his powerful gaze.

"You did not . . ." he gasps. He grips her elbows sharply and pulls her towards him fiercely, his grey eyes glinting in anger. "You *cannot*. You hear me? You *cannot* fall in love with me."

"Let me go!" she forces out, wriggling her hand out of his grasp. Once she pulls her hand away, she rubs her wrists and glares at him. "You can't tell me what to do. It's a *feeling*. You can't control feelings!"

"You can't fall in love with me!" he says but this time it's not in anger. It's out desperation. His hoodie's has fallen off his head and he's running his hands through his black hair. Carmen bites her lip and looks around to see if anyone in the beach saw him but it looked almost empty.

"You . . ." he swallows thickly. "Why—I—You can't. You shouldn't. This is not good. Carmen, there's—I'm—how can you fall in love with me?" he asks desperately. He looked like a crumbled mess, weak and torn.

"You want me to apologise for falling in love with you?" she asks incredulously. "This—"

"No!" he says loudly. "No! I'm asking you *how*. *How* can you fall in love with me? Can you even imagine a life with me?"

"You don't really think about anything when you fall in love," she mutters.

"Well, maybe you should!" he cries. "You should because that's what matters. I come from a different place. *I* am Death. Can you see what you've done? You've fallen in love with Death!"

"You think I wanted this?" she fumes.

"Carmen, this is not a joke! You can't just fall in love with people. It's like you're trying so desperately to make your life miserable. Do you know what you're saying? Do you know how absurd it sounds? Do you know the trouble you could get in to?"

"I—"

"You know what?" Jeroën stands up, dusting off the sand from his shorts. He pulls up his hoodie and looks at her fiercely. "I can't do this anymore."

The waves are louder.

"You humans are so stupid.

WHOOSH.

"I can't believe that you would do something absurd like this!"

SPLASH.

"We should just stop seeing each other."

CRASH.

"It was nice meeting you, Carmen Collins."

WHOOSH.

"You're a great person and thank you for making my stay memorable."

SPLASH.

He turns around and walks a few steps away from her but he turns back and gives her a mocking smile, like he always used to. "Have a good day."

CRASH.

• • •

"Wow. This is awesome."

"Yeah. Sorry about yes—"

"You apologised like a million times. I told you, it's okay."

"Um, so, I don't have a gift for you," she says blushing. She's wearing a white frock and her blonde hair is left loose in ringlets. Adrian almost felt like he was dreaming when he first saw her. "But," she continues, "Akelard told me about your obsession with stars and it seems almost absurd that you don't know a thing about constellations so that's what I'm going to do!"

"You're going to teach me about constellations . . .?"

"Yeah," she winces. "I wanted to get you something but I'm broke."

He chuckles. "It's fine, really."

"In a way, I'm actually gifting you a memory."

". . . Okay . . ."

Adrian and Sheila are seated on the edge of a cliff with their legs dangling. It was a short cliff that was about ten feet above the ground. Sheila had remained mute the entire time they drove to this place that was quite a distance behind her building.

Adrian felt that he could spend hours and hours listening to Sheila babble on and on about stars and constellations. Nothing really made sense but yet, it did. He felt like instead of connecting stars, he could stare at them and wonder if their futures would be entwined together like tight vines.

"I love you," he finally says in a breathy whisper.

She stops talking. She freezes and slowly veers her head towards him. "What?"

"I said I love you," he says with a slow smile.

Her usually bright brown eyes loosen their glow. With shivering lips, she mutters, "What kind of sick joke is this?"

Now, Adrian had expected a lot of things. Excitement, astonishment, happiness but rejection was not one of them. His face pales as he shakes his head. "It's not."

She jolts up like an electric shock coursed through her spine. She breathes heavily and says, "Do you have *any* idea of what you're saying?"

"Sheila, I—"

"You what? You think it's cute to *fall in love* with the daughter of a higher, a supreme being?"

"What? Hey listen—"

"No. You listen to me. This is bad, okay? This is . . . impossible and . . . unthinkable!" she exclaims, tears running down her face. "Why do you have to ruin everything?"

He doesn't say anything except look up at the stars, biting the insides of his cheek. For once, the stars don't comfort him.

"You know what?" She wipes her face with her hands. "Forget it. Go home, it's late. Good night."

• • •

Chapter 30

Adrian Feels Numb

At this moment, he doesn't know what anger is. He doesn't know what sadness is. As he feels the breeze gently kiss his tanned skin, he feels nothing. It's strange because he's supposed to be crying his eyes out.

He wonders if this is peace. He can hear his heartbeat in his ears and he likes how it goes *thump-a-thump.* He likes how his head s rejecting the thought of her. He tries to think about what happened. What happened? Was she sad? Was she pissed?

It's all a blur and he can't remember anything.

And he doesn't mind it. Seated on a swing in the beach, he felt light and he decided to let it be. He could see girls winking at him and he smiles politely back at them.

He looks up at the blue sky and after a few minutes, he stands up, picks up his diving board and he heads to the blue sea with a jovial smile on his face, his curls bouncing with every step he takes.

• • •

Carmen tries to scrub away her pain.

She runs her skin violently with her loofah. It was funny how she thought that his presence was all over her body. She scrubs her skin as though the memories were dirt on her skin. She feels dirty, used and wasted.

"My fault," she cries as water washes away the suds. It is then that Carmen realises that she's not fearless and no one is. She realises that she was scared of her flaws. Sure, she wasn't scared of spiders or heights or closed spaces but she was scared of the person she was slowly becoming. She didn't like feeling like a stranger in her own body. She didn't like how light her eyes were. She didn't like her skinny arms and legs.

She didn't like herself.

Her heartbeat is drowned by her loud cries and she does not try to stop. Her tears come out like a flowing river of pain and anguish. After her shower, she feels cleaner, relieved.

Carmen's looks at the mirror and smiles softly at her reflection.

• • •

"Ugh, no offence to Omar but I told you about his mom right? So bloody judgmental. The last time I met her, she told me I looked fat in my cocktail dress when in reality, I *did not*," Layla blabbers.

Carmen rolls her eyes as she curls another stand of Layla's brunette hair. "But you love Omar. So you'll do this for him, right?"

"That I will."

Meanwhile, in the other room, Adrian's watching Omar fret with his tie.

"Dude, you don't know my parents. They completely disapprove of my relationship with Layla and she has to set an impression this time. I hope Carmen knows what she's doing."

"Chill," Adrian drawls. "She knows what she's doing. You guys will look great."

And they did. As they stood together, smiling uncertainly at their three friends who stood before them.

Layla, who was certain that Omar's mother approved of collared dresses, wore a red dress that had black velvet collars. She had a rose gold bracelet and necklace on and *because* Omar felt that his dad hated stilettos, she wore black flat on. Omar wore a simple black suit with a white shirt and black tie.

"You guys look great," Akelard said with a smile. "Akelard approves."

"I feel like I should take photos of you two and it's not even prom," Carmen chuckles. "You guys will do great."

"I share the same sentiment."

After the couple is ushered out, Akelard forces the two of them to sit down and because they were too tired to protest, they did.

He claps his hands and grins. "You know, remember I told you about a guy I like in Für Elise?"

Carmen and Adrian nod lazily.

"He asked me out!"

". . . He did?" Adrian asks.

"Yeah! And we're going on a date tomorrow!"

"That's . . . great," Carmen says with a slow smile.

But they watch sourly as he waltzes around the room.

• • •

"What did he say?"

"That he didn't expect me to do something like that."

"Huh."

"What did she say?"

"That it was wrong and I ruined everything."

"Ouch."

"Nicholas Sparks didn't teach me how to deal with rejection."

"I'm pretty sure that his books are all tragedies?"

"..."

"..."

"..."

"..."

They roll their eyes and chuckle.

•••

Chapter 31

Carmen Doesn't Look Up

The diagrams in her book suddenly appear interesting and she wonders why she never looked at them before. Funny how she had to take notice of these things in uncomfortable situations.

He clears his throat again. "Carmen?"

She still doesn't look up. She can feel his dominating presence around her and it's making her nervous. She clenches her sweaty palms and inhales deeply.

"Carmen."

This time she looks up because she can hear desperation in his voice. She looks up and meets his grey eyes. Jeroën looks tired, with dark circles around his eyes and his face looks droopy.

"Can I talk to you?"

"Aren't you doing that right now?"

"No—I mean," he sighs an annoyed sigh. "Can I sit next to you?"

She shrugs. "It's a lecture theatre. I don't have any claim over any of the seats. Do whatever you want."

He clenches his jaw but his steely gaze doesn't make her cower. She feels better like for once, she has the situation under control. He slumps on the seat next to her. They're the only ones in the Physics lecture theatre.

Jeroën fiddles with his thumbs while Carmen resumes with her work. His presence bothers her and she hopes he doesn't notice her feverishly stealing glances at him.

Finally, he sighs loudly. "I want to talk about what happened on Friday."

"What happened on Friday?"

"Stop that, Carmen. I'm serious."

She shuts her book and turns to him. "Okay, what?"

"I . . . thought about what I said and I . . . was too brash. I'm sorry. I wasn't thinking straight but . . . in a way, what I said was—"

"You accused me for falling in love with you."

". . . I did."

She smiles a little as he hangs his head down in shame like a child who got caught for doing something wrong. "Look Jeroën. I wish I could that I'm sorry but I really can't. I know you can't love me because you're Death. I know and it doesn't bother me one bit because loving you has made me realise so much about myself that I was too dense to see. I never knew love was this powerful," she chuckles slightly and says," I wish you knew how it felt."

"Carmen, I—"

"I'm nothing special, Jeroën. I'm not fearless. I'm scared of my insecurities. I'm scared if anybody will find out about them. I'm scared of you but you know what? Unlike the others, I accept reality and I assume that's the only way I can see you like how I see you. I know that one day I'll die." She tucks in a strand of her red hair under her hair band and says, "I'm not fearless."

After letting out her feelings, she looks up at Jeroën's eyes. His usually smug or emotionless look is gone. Instead, he looks troubled.

"Jeroën, how the hell—"

He starts to cough fiercely. He stands up quickly and rushes, "I—I have to go!"

But Carmen didn't miss how red his usually pale face went.

•••

"So, *today,* I'm in college and oh my God, I'm so excited to show you guys how it's like. Like literally, college is *so* much fun. Let me show you my friends!" Michelin giggles. She places the camera in front of Adrian and says, "So *guys,* this is my bestie, Adrian! Isn't he *so* cute?"

"What the . . . fuck?" Adrian frowns as she comes closer with her camera. "What are you doing?"

"Guys, my bestie just cursed! Isn't that like . . . so cute?"

"What—"

"Adrian says hi to my YouTube subscribers!"

Adrian screws his eyebrows together in confusion. "You're what?"

"Aw guys, he doesn't know what I'm talking about! Isn't that so cute?!"

"What are you doing?"

Michelin giggles again. "I'm vlogging."

"Well, leave me out of it." He stands up and slings his bag over his shoulder.

She lets out an annoyed hiss and follows him, shoving her camera in the pocket of her shorts. "You just ruined my YouTube video!"

"Sorry," he says lazily. He pulls out is sunglasses from the pocket of his shirt and puts it on. "You were invading my privacy."

When he feels like she's gone, he lets out a relieved sigh. He likes walking in the college grounds particularly when it's almost empty. He likes basking in the sunlight with no one to bother him.

He sticks his hands into his pockets, whistling some tune. He steps on a few dried up leaves that are in his path liking the feel and sound of the leaves crunching under his heel. Soon, he can hear footsteps synchronising his own. Adrian chuckles under his breath and slows his pace. He stops and swivels around.

"You're stalking me."

She smiles sheepishly, her red lips stretching. She pushes up her glasses and sighs. "I am."

"And, to what do I owe the pleasure of the daughter of . . . Iudex stalk me?"

Sheila tightens her jaw. She looks like summer in her yellow shirt and white skirt with her hair loose. "I need to talk to you."

"Who's stopping you?"

She lets out a heavy sigh, pinching the bridge of her nose. "Don't be like that, Adrian."

He softens the sharpness in his voice and asks, "What is it, Sheila?"

"I . . . I wanted to apologise for the way I acted that night. I was . . . brash and stupid and I don't know what I was thinking, I swear—"

"Okay, whoa, you're saying a lot of words and I don't understand anything—"

"All you need to know is that," she takes a deep breath, "I was wrong."

Adrian furrows his eyebrows in confusion. "What?"

"I," she gulps. Adrian can see beads of sweat forming on her forehead. "I . . . I can't deny how I feel. I'm not a Death. I can feel. I wish I could just . . . I wish I could just tell you!"

"What is it?"

"I love you."

It was then that Adrian had reached the zenith of his life. He felt a flush of emotions flush through his body and he could swear on everything he owned that he was in a different world. He remembers his dad telling him how love felt like. How it was an assurance at time of desperation. How it's like a drop of water to a person who's thirsty. How it's like an umbrella on a hot day.

Adrian was sure of it. This is love.

• • •

Chapter 32

Adrian Sips His Glass of Wine

"My first kiss," Adrian says, shoving a forkful of salad into his mouth, "was with a guy."

"*What?*"

"Yeah," he cringes. "The guy was drunk and it was forced. Yup, not much to talk about."

Sheila nods. "I wish I could relate. But I can't."

"Thank you. That makes me feel a lot better."

"You're welcome," she says. "I'm known for my sympathising ear . . ."

Adrian laughs. "Really?"

". . . and my helpful advice so, you should be proud that you're on a date with me," she says, placing her hand on her chest.

They chatter a lot. In her black sleeveless dress with polka dotted tights, Adrian can't stop staring at her and he doesn't think that he will ever get tired of her.

After dinner, they decide to walk home instead of hollering for a cab.

"You liked it, I hope?" Adrian asks, tightening the shawl around his neck.

"I did," she smiles. "Here," she hands him her bag, "hold this for a minute." She puts on her red knee length coat. "Thanks."

A few minutes of silence pass by in which they could only hear the clacking of their shoes. Adrian clicks his tongue to lessen the awkwardness of the situation. Sheila twiddles her thumbs.

"Why are you so fidgety?"

She looks up, startled. Coughing nervously, she shakes her head. "What do you mean?"

He stops walking and raises his eyebrow. "I was noticing you during our date. You were very . . . tensed and nervous like someone's . . . forcing you to be here."

"Uh . . . no?"

"Uh . . . yes?" Arian says, imitating her dubious expression. "You were really tensed and disturbed. What's up?"

Sheila shakes her head, her blonde ringlets bouncing. "I just . . . we're going to get into a lot of trouble by doing this. This isn't allowed and my father knows everything. He'll find out about this in no time and . . . I just don't want to pull you into danger."

"You won't," he says in a soothing whisper, cupping her cheek. "I promise you won't."

She heaves a sigh, rubbing the crease between her eyebrows. "I hope so. C'mon, let's go."

• • •

"How did the date go?"

Sheila looks up and smiles brightly. "It was great. I had fun."

Carmen nods and shuts her book. She pushes it to the corner of the table and puts her pens and pencils on top of it. She pushes her hair back and ties it into a loose bun.

"Architecture looks tiring."

"It is. Ugh, I have a horrible headache coming."

"Do you want me to get some aspirin for you?"

"That would be awesome. There's a container on the first drawer of the shoe rack. Could you get me it?"

Sheila pushes back her chair and jogs up to the shoe rack. She almost topples off the flower vase that's placed on top of the shoe rack as she runs her fingers through all the small plastic containers in the drawer.

Hearing the ruckus, Carmen leans back in her chair and hollers, "You okay there?"

"I'm fine!" She grasps the container and shuts the drawer. Sheila walks into the kitchen and gets a jug of water. She fills a glass with water and takes it to Carmen's room.

"Here," he says in a hushed whisper and places the glass and container on the table. Carmen smiles gratefully and takes a huge gulp of water and pops in the pill before gulping the contents.

Sheila bites her lip and says slowly, "I . . . know what happened."

Carmen places the glass on the table and furrows her eyebrows. "What happened?"

She bites the insides of her cheek. "Um, you know, between you and Jeroën."

"Adrian told you?"

"No. Jeroën did."

"He would," she says bitterly and sniffs. "He definitely would."

"It's just that . . . it's—it won't work out because," she sighs, "it's impossible. Has Jeroën told you about the 1500 incident?"

Carmen rolls her eyes. "Yeah. Some bullshit about a Death falling in love with a girl and how later on, he was tortured until the feelings were ripped off of him and how the girl committed suicide."

"*That's* what he told you?" she asks incredulously.

"No. I just gave you a summary of it."

"I'm terribly sorry. You know, what's going on between Adrian and me is prohibited too and I'm going to land in a lot of trouble because of it but . . . this is too real. This is way too real."

"I know," Carmen says slowly with a sad smile. "I can see that but it's *fine.* I don't know what I expecting, to be honest. But hey," she leans closer. "Can I ask you something?"

"Shoot."

"Uh, when Jeroën came to me yesterday and apologised, he was acting really weird."

"What . . . do you mean?"

"He actually went red. Like his skin, you know how pale it is. It went red and he was super nervous."

". . ."

"Also, when he got teased by a couple of people in college, you should've seen him. He looked . . . hurt and insecure."

Sheila shakes her head. "Are you sure?"

"Yeah. Yeah, I am," Carmen says, vigorously nodding her head. "Is he alright?"

Sheila pales. "I don't know. It definitely doesn't sound right."

• • •

Chapter 33

Carmen Feels Overwhelmed

"*What?*" she yells at the screen.

"I know, I know!" he wails, shaking his head. "She actually told that to me."

"That's horrible!"

"Thank you," he says flatly. "That makes me feel a lot better."

"Sorry," she smiles sheepishly. "But you haven't told me *exactly* what she said. What did she say? Like the exact words."

"'I'm not the right girl for you and you deserve so much better than me. I don't have the privilege to be in your destiny and you're smart and awesome but I found someone else,'" Markus says in a high pitched voice. He scowls and says, "The nerve she had!"

Carmen bites her lip and says, "Who is the . . . guy?"

"My roommate!"

"Okay, Markus, it's fine. It's all for the best, alright? I never really liked Elle, to be honest."

"You're telling me this now?"

"I've told this to you the minute you guys got together!"

"Anyways," he says combing his blonde hair with his fingers. "It's funny how you and I go through such tragedies in the same time."

"Yeah," she snorts, "real funny."

"What was the guy's name again?"

"Jeroën Jarvis."

"I don't know why but the name sounds very fancy."

"Yeah," she says shrugging. "He's a fancy guy."

"Well, who cares, right? Like you said, it's for the best and who knows? Maybe our soul mates," he says dramatically fanning himself with a paper, "are out there searching for us."

"Maybe," she lets out a fake chuckle.

• • •

"Coming!" she yells and shoves the kitchen mop against the shelf. She wipes her wet hands on her apron and rushes to open the door.

"Jeroën?"

"Hi," he gasps, heavily breathing. "I rang the bell for a long time. Where were you?"

"Cooking, cleaning the kitchen . . ." she trails, running her eyes over his flushed face. His face is moist and red with sweat. "Are you okay?"

"I'm okay. Can I come in?"

"Sure." She moves aside and closes the door softly after he gets in. "Um, so, why the unexpected visit?"

"No reason," he says, smiling nervously. He peels off his cardigan and Carmen tries not to stare at the swirling names on his arms.

"Are you okay? You haven't been acting like yourself lately," she says as he slumps on a nearby couch.

"I'm fine," he frowns like as though his body was rejecting the word. He gives a forced smile and says, "I found out that your birthday's next week."

"Oh yeah. November 7th. That's on Tuesday, I think?"

"It is. Why didn't you tell me?"

"I'm not so big on birthdays," she shrugs. "To be honest, I forgot about it."

Jeroën looks at her with an expression that she can't decipher. "What do you want for your birthday?"

"Nothing really. You don't have to get me anything. Just come for dinner."

His grey eyes make her feel self conscious. "You must want something."

"You're right," she says seriously. "But it's something you can't give me."

He narrows his eyes. "And what's that?"

"For you to love me and have babies with me," she says giving a fake sniff.

"What?"

"I'm kidding! Gee, take a joke would you?"

"That's not very funny," he scowls. "That's a horrible joke."

"That hurts my feelings. A lot."

"Boohoo."

"I made some hot chocolate," she says with a flat look. "Do you want some?"

He shrugs, his grey eyes smouldering into hers. "Fine."

She gives him a short smile and walks to her kitchen. Carmen pulls out two mugs and pours out hot chocolate into them. She puts on her kitchen gloves and winds her fingers through the handles and carries it gingerly to Jeroën. He straightens up when he sees her coming. She smiles again and says, "Careful, it's hot."

"That's why it's called hot chocolate."

"Shut up, smartass. Here." She hands him his mug and accidentally brushes her fingers with him.

Jeroën stares at her as she blushes and takes a huge gulp of her hot chocolate.

• • •

"Sheila, what's wrong?"

She bangs the door with her fist.

"Sheila, stop—"

Carmen opens the door with a scowl. "Who's dying over here?"

Sheila pushes past her roughly. Carmen stumbles by the door and gives Adrian a quizzical look. "What's wrong?"

Adrian steps in the apartment and whispers, "I don't know. She's been acting really fidgety through the movie."

"Where's he?" Sheila snaps, looking at Carmen angrily.

"Who . . . are you talking about?"

"Jeroën! Who else?"

"He's—"

As if on cue, Jeroën appears from the kitchen with a bewildered expression. He looks at Sheila and instantly, guilt's all over his face.

"Come here," she snarls and grabs him by his elbow and she marches towards Adrian's room, dragging Jeroën behind her.

"What the hell?"

"What's going on?" Carmen asks Adrian. "Why's she all worked up?"

"I have no idea," he says shaking his head. "You should've seen her in the theatre. Like, I wasn't watching movie. I was just watching her acting all angry and flustered."

From his room, a lot of yelling could be heard. Carmen makes a move towards the room but she's pulled back by Adrian who gives her a mortified look.

"That's bad manners! You're not eavesdropping!"

". . ."

"Fine," he frowns. "But I don't approve of it."

"Who cares?" she mutters and they tiptoe to the room. They press their index fingers to their lips and press their ears to the door.

"What the hell do you think is happening?" Sheila cries. "This is wrong!"

"You think I don't know that?" Jeroën says. Carmen doesn't like how helpless he sounds. "You think I don't know that? You think I like this? You think I want this? I don't want this!"

"You'll be in Purgatory in no time, Jeroën!" she snarls. "Do you think my father won't see the changes in you? You think he'll let it go."

"I know your father more than you do," he says in a lower tone. "I know him more than you do and I know what I'm going to go through."

"Do you know how *human* you sound?"

" . . ."

"I don't want you to end up in trouble. Most importantly, I don't want Carmen to get into trouble. She's involving in a sphere that's believed to be fictional."

"She's a foolish girl," Jeroën mutters. Adrian snickers and Cramen nudges his shoulder roughly. "She doesn't know love."

"And you do?" she retorts.

"I . . . don't."

"Jeroën, we've talked about this."

Carmen presses her ear firmly against the door only to be pulled back roughly by Adrian who drags her to the den. He pushes her to a couch and says, "Do you know what this means?"

"No . . . ? Why did you bring me all the way here to tell me that?" she asks and lets out an annoyed sigh. "Come, let's go."

"Carmen," he snaps. "This means that Jeroën's turning into a person he's not supposed to be."

"He's not a person," Carmen says, rolling her eyes. "He's Death."

" . . ."

"*No* way."

"In this case, *yes* way."

• • •

Chapter 34

Adrian Hits Her with a Pillow Again

"Stop!" she yells, her voice muffled by the comforter.

"Carmen, wake up!" he says jovially, hitting her again. "It's your birthday, you dumbass."

"Okay, fine. So, leave me alone!"

"Payback's a bitch."

"Get off me. I can't breathe."

"But it's your birthday."

"So, you want to kill me?" she groans.

"It's my birthday," he sings, "it's my birthday and I'm gonna spend some money—"

"It's *my* birthday," she says flatly, pulling the covers off her head. Her red hair is a crumpled mess but Adrian always liked it when her hair was messy. "And stop singing that song. It's annoying and stupid."

"Get *up.*"

"How am I supposed to get up? You're on me," she scowls.

He gets off her and spreads himself on her bed. "Get ready quick. Omar, Lay and Akelard are here."

"They are?" she yawns, stretching her arms. Adrian tries not to snicker at her Barbie pyjamas. "When did they come?"

"A few minutes back," he shrugs. "They got cake. Hurry up."

Carmen stumbles sleepily to the bathroom and takes a quick shower. She rubs her eyes and puts on a white shirt and burgundy red skirt. She ties her red wet hair into a loose bun and sticks in a few pins.

She walks into her room to see Adrian flicking through some magazine. He looks up and grins wildly. "You look great!"

"Thanks," she mutters. "I told you that you didn't have to do all this. It's just a birthday."

"Birthdays are like the only reason to celebrate."

"It's just a reminder that you survived another shitty year."

"You're *so* pessimistic. C'mon."

• • •

"He drew me!"

"That's not fair," Adrian grumbles. "He gave me a book on how to cook and he sketches a portrait of you. So unfair."

"You were the one getting all hyped up over my birthday," she snorts. "Look at you now."

"Just check the gift," he snaps. Carmen sticks out her tongue playfully and proceeds to rip out Uncle Joe's gift.

"A watch," she says softly. "He got me a watch."

"Not bad. You get a diamond bracelet from Akelard, a twenty dollar gift card from Omar which was expected, a dress from Layla, a set of earrings from my dad," Adrian says with an appreciative nod. "This is like the best you've ever gotten."

"Wow," she says sarcastically. "Thanks a lot."

"You're welcome," he grins. "My gift is comparatively shit, to be honest."

"What is it?"

Adrian shrugs and gets up from the couch. He steps on all the wrappers and jogs to his room. He pulls out a wrapped box from the drawer and just out his lip in confusion. After contemplating a lot, he rips out the wrapper and pulls out the contents.

"She hates my wrapping anyway," he mutters.

When Adrian hands it to her, she smiles brightly and her eyes hine in wonder. "You got me a Polaroid!"

"I did," he smiles. "You kept telling me about how much you wanted it so I got it."

"And . . ." she trails, getting out a pink box. "You got me a . . . *no*."

"Pretty cool, eh?" he smirks.

"You teased Akelard a lot when he got me that diamond bracelet," she snaps. "But you got me Tiffany & Co. Earrings!"

"I did," he says proudly.

"You're so fucking weird."

"I'm so fucking cool is what I am."

• • •

"Tell him to get out."

"Don't be rude, Adrian," she says. "Why don't you go talk to Shila or something? I'll talk to him, alright?"

Adrian gives Jeroën a nasty glare. Everyone in the den gapes at Jeroën's arrival. Carmen smiles at them and says, "You guys can continue doing what you were doing. Jeroën will be here only for some time."

Layla coughs. "Why? You can join us and have cake. I made it so," she scoffs, "it'll be pretty great."

"I'm sure," Jeroën says politely. "But I can't stay for too long."

Carmen can see how hard Layla tries to hide her grimace when he smiles at her. She doesn't miss the hard glare Sheila shoots at him when she ushers him into the kitchen.

"I'm sorry about that. Adrian—"

"—hates me. I know. I came to wish you actually."

"Oh. Oh okay. Uh . . ."

"Happy Birthday," he chuckles. "You're awkward as always."

They stare at each other. Carmen notices how tired and drawn out he looks. His skin in not pale anymore. His skin is tanned.

"Jeroën," she sighs, "are you okay? You don't look well."

"You think that I'm sick?" he snorts.

"No," she says with a thin air of patience. "What I think is that you're not acting and looking like yourself."

"Look," he says and clicks his tongue. "I . . . I have to tell you something."

"What is it?"

"Uh . . . okay. Look I—"

The kitchen door is slammed open and Adrian walks in with Sheila. "Get out, Jeroën."

"I just want to—"

"Get out, Jeroën," Sheila says softly. "If you know what's good for you."

Jeroën clenches his jaw and before parting, he gives Carmen a smile and Carmen could swear that his hands were shivering.

•••

Chapter 35

Carmen Straightens Her Blue Skirt

"What are you fretting for?" Layla asks, squinting in the sunlight.

"It's nothing," Carmen shrugs trying to seem nonchalant. "Uh . . . you guys happen to see Jeroën?"

Omar and Layla exchange a weary look. "What for?" Omar asks, cocking an eyebrow.

"Just because."

"That doesn't answer the question," Layla says folding her arms. "Are you guys a thing or something?"

"W—what?!" she splutters almost dropping her coffee. "Where's that coming from?"

"The other week, at your birthday, you guys kind of kicked him out," she says, pursing her lips. "So . . . I gathered that some kind of—"

"Nothing of that sort happened," Carmen says quickly. "Nope. Just . . . where is he?"

"I didn't see him," Omar says tightening the belt around his coat, "which is weird because we had our exam today."

"Exactly," Carmen muses, rubbing her chin. "Something's up."

"Well, *Sherlock,* it doesn't matter. Our exams just got over and here you are, worrying about that . . . guy."

"Shut up, Lay."

"Carmen," Layla says. "We have a music—"

"—festival tonight," Carmen says flatly. "I know. You don't have to keep telling me that."

• • •

He feels the sand tickle his toes.

Layla had lied. It wasn't a music festival. It was just a gathering of the Art student in her college where they played music and sold their artwork. Nevertheless, Adrian liked the atmosphere.

He could hear happiness in the music that was played by a couple of guys. Sheila and he were seated away from the crowd on some mound of sand. Sheila (being a neat freak) didn't want to sit on sand so Adrian forced her to sit on his lap.

Adrian presses a kiss on her head, softly breathing in her vanilla scent.

"I like this," Sheila breathes, placing her hand on Adrian's knee. "This is nice."

"Isn't it?" he mutters, placing another kiss on her head. She turns towards him and smiles softly. He leans in and kisses her.

Kissing Sheila felt like tasting his dreams. That feeling he would get, that feeling when his heart would start to beat fast and his head felt light was how he felt when he kissed Sheila. He could taste love on the tip of his tongue and there was nothing more he wanted than to kiss Sheila under the blanket of a thousand stars.

A cold breeze blows by but Adrian feels warm with Sheila in his arms.

• • •

"So, you guys spent the entire time making out?"

"No."

"That's why you ditched us?" Carmen asks and gives a fake sniff. "That's nice, Adrian."

"Thank you," Adrian says and does a curtsy. "I outdo myself at times."

Carmen pours herself some coffee from the kettle and sips it. Adrian shakes his eyebrow and points at the clock. "You're drinking coffee and it's midnight. You okay in the head?"

She makes a face at him and continues to sip her coffee. "You know," she says sneaking a look at him as he browses in his laptop, "you look really happy."

"That's because I—"

There's a knock at the door.

Carmen gets up from her bean bag chair and places her cup of coffee on a table. She walks over to the door and unlocks it.

"Carmen," Jeroën gasps pushing himself in. He shuts the door loudly by pressing his back against it and wipes the sweat on his forehead. "Carmen."

"Who the—" starts Adrian. When he sees the intruder, he folds his arms and says, "Get out."

"Adrian," snaps Carmen. "Shut up." She looks at Jeroën and peers at Jeroën's face and asks, "Why . . . are you so . . . tired?"

"I" —he gasps— "can't! I—there's something wrong."

"What?"

"I'm leaving to Purgatory in two days," he says in one breath.

"Thank God," Adrian gives out a relived sigh.

"Adrian, what is your issue?" Carmen snaps.

"Cars—"

"Shut up!" she turns to Jeroën. "Why are you telling this to me now?"

"I just came to know," he gulps. Carmen can see his Adam's apple bobbing up and down as he takes deep breaths.

"So, I'll never see you again?"

"No."

Carmen feels horrible. Like something worse is going to come. "Jeroën . . . do you want to tell me something?"

Jeroën nods stiffly. He peels off his cardigan and gestures Carmen to come closer. She leans in. He points at the vein on his hand that's still in black italics.

Carmen Collins.

"No," she gasps, falling to her knees. "Me . . . no!"

And on that instant, she saw what everyone else so. She saw Jeroën as an awkwardly short guy with white hair. She saw his crooked eyebrows. She saw his stuck up nose. She could *feel* the power.

She saw Death like the others and she was scared.

"Yes," he whispers softly. "You're my first soul to take when I go back to Purgatory."

• • •

Chapter 36

Adrian Feels Like a Bucket of Cold Water is Thrown at Him

He shudders at first like as though the name was whispered like a breeze into his ear.

"Is this a fucking joke?" he snarls, inching closer to Jeroën who looks guiltily at the floor. He clutches the collars of Jeroën's shirt and pulls him closer. For the first time, he doesn't waver at the alarming power in Jeroën's eyes.

"Adrian—"

"Is it a joke?!" he yells.

He looks down and sighs, "No."

Adrian lets go of his collars only to pull back his fist and punch his face. He pulls back his fist and tries to ignore the stinging pain in his fist. Jeroën looks flatly at him which angers him even more.

"*What is your problem?*" he yells. "Why do you keep—"

"I'm sorry, I'm sorry, I'm sorry," Jeroën mutters clenching his eyes shut. "I'm so sorry."

"Why do *you* have to ruin it? You can't just fucking take her soul!"

"You think I can control this?" Jeroën spits back, his grey eyes blazing with fury. Adrian takes a step back as he glares at him. "You make me look like the culprit when I'm not even the culprit."

"Carmen—" Adrian turns to see Carmen on the floor.

• • •

She wakes up to blinding light.

She squints a few times before opening her blue eyes widely. Adrian is seated on the edge of the bed with his head in his arms. Carmen can make out that he's crying because his shoulders are shaking profusely.

"Adrian."

He looks up alert. He snaps his head towards her and grins widely. He leaps over to her and engulfs her in a tight hug. "You're okay, you're okay."

Carmen tries to be light hearted. She pulls back and looks at him flatly. "You thought I was dead? You're not going to get rid of me so easily."

"Stop . . ." Adrian falters but he shakes his head. "Stop acting."

"What should I do then?" Carmen asks. "Should I cry? Moan and lament about it? It's bound to happen sometime."

"How can you be optimistic and brave?" Adrian cries. Carmen feels guilty at the sight of the tears streaming down his face. He wipes it quickly and shakes his head furiously. "You can't leave. I have so many more memories to share with you."

Carmen bites her lip and tries to keep her emotion in check. "I'm pretty sure you can't control that."

"You can't go," Adrian whispers. His curls are arranged messily and she runs her fingers through it. "You're the only one who understands me. You can't just leave me like that."

At that moment, she doesn't hold it back. Memories of how he finished up all her cookies even though they were half burnt when they first met flushes through her. Nights when they would go up to Adrian's terrace or to the beach to look up at stars fills her head and she feels dizzy. "I don't want to go," Carmen whispers, tears falling down. "I don't want to go."

"I don't think I can handle reality without you, Cars," Adrian cries. "I can't."

• • •

He sniffs in his sleep.

Carmen checks again. When she's sure that he's asleep, she pushes the covers away from her body and puts on her slippers. She opens the door to a point where she was sure it would not creak and squeezes herself through the small space.

Once she was sure she was out and Adrian wouldn't detect her absence, she walks stealthily to the den where she was sure he would be and sees him sitting on a couch, staring at a wall.

"Hey," she whispers softly. Jeroën looks up and stands up, his eyes wide.

"You're awake!" he says with a wide grin.

"I am," she says and sits on the couch. She pats the spot next to her and says, "Sit."

He sits down and stares at her as though he was evaluating her.

"What?"

"You don't have to act like you're not affected by the news. It's okay to be terrified," Jeroën says. "I was when I got your name."

She raises an eyebrow. "You were?"

"Yeah."

"Why? I thought you were immune to feelings?" she asks. "What changed?"

He clenches his jaw. "You don't know what you're talking about."

Carmen shrugs. "Fine. You know, when you told me that I was going to die, I actually saw you like how the others saw you."

"Yeah?"

"Uh huh. You looked pretty gross with white hair and a stuck up nose," she says wrinkling her nose. "No wonder everyone's so repulsive towards you."

He chuckles. "Do I look the same?"

She shakes her head slowly, her eyes raking over his black hair and defined jaw. "Nope. Definitely not. I have to ask you something."

"What's it?"

"How am I supposed to die? Don't you know that?"

Jeroën takes a sharp intake of breath. "I do. You're actually supposed to die in a fire."

"What?" Carmen whispers hoarsely. "I'm going to be burnt to death?"

"Look," Jeroën says with a determined expression. "I can make it easy for you. I'll get into trouble but I already am in trouble so it's not going to change much. Do you know that spare room on the top floor?"

"Yeah . . . it's locked though."

"Hm," he nods. "You will be there on Sunday. The door is unlocked and you will enter it. There will be a gas cylinder in there which you think is empty but it's on. You light a lighter—"

"Why am I lighting a lighter?" Carmen asks incredulously.

"Because the light will go off and you won't bring a torch with you because you will lose it. Adrian will put a lighter in the kitchen. At that time, you will be having a mental breakdown so you will not think much. You will take the lighter with you."

"Oh God. Now that I know this, I can stop it, right?"

"You can't meddle with fate. If you do, it'll end up pretty bad. It's planned, Carmen. It's your fate. I can which is why I'm telling you that I can make it quick. I can change the way you will die. I'll take your soul and it will be only a matter of seconds—"

"Don't talk like that!" she snaps. "You're talking about my death."

"You will *burn* to death," Jeroën says leaning in closer. "Do you want that?"

". . . no . . ."

"So, it's better that we do it my way."

"Won't this get you into trouble with Iudex and Per—Per?"

"*Percontator,*" Jeroën chuckles. "I told you before. I already am in trouble. Nothing's going to change that."

"What are you in trouble for?"

"I can't tell you that," he says quickly.

"Fine," she sighs and in a softer tone she adds, "Uh Jeroën?"

"Don't," he says looking at her. "Please don't."

"I don't want to leave!" she says exasperatedly. "I can't leave Adrian."

"This is fate," he says shaking his head. "I told you. You can't meddle with fate."

"Fuck you fate," she mutters.

• • •

Chapter 37

Carmen Says Her Goodbye

She presses a small kiss on Adrian forehead. He stirs a little as Carmen's tears fall on his cheek. She hisses in annoyance and wipes it off gently.

She closes the door behind her. She looks around the apartment again and somewhere in her head, she feels a deep sense of longing to call Uncle Joe, to see Omar, Layla and Akelard. But she doesn't. Instead, she puts on her cardigan and gets the keys. She unlocks the door and steps out gingerly.

"Oh God," she whispers, tasting her salty tears. "She puts on her crocs and passes by Akelard's apartment. She closes her eyes for a minute and then with a deep breath, she walks up the stairs.

Lucky for her, they lived in the 10th floor which means that she just had to walk two floors. When she arrives at the last floor, she gulps. She walks across the corridor.

She's whimpering as she drags herself to the last room in the corridor. The door's paint had come off. She clutches the door knob with a shivering hand. It's pushed open with a creak and she steps in. An eerie silence fills the room. She shuts the door behind her and looks around.

The room has an old shelf at one corner of the room and a flickering bulb in the middle of the room. There are tables and chair on top of the tables in another corner of the room. There're large French windows and Carmen can feel her feet pulling her towards the windows. She places her hands on the windows and gapes at the sight.

Streetlights illuminate the inky blackness of the night sky. She can see cars speeding along the highway, couples and children walking on the sidewalk. She can hear faint noises of laughter and giggles.

She turns away and presses her back against the cold glass.

Carmen can hear a voice in her head, something that compels her to sit down. So, she pulls out a chair from the bunch of chairs and drags it to the centre of the room. As if on cue, the light flickers out.

She tries to calm herself by singing an Amy Winehouse song in her head as she sits down. She straightens her shirt and folds her hands on her lap. She doesn't know what she's waiting for. Is she waiting for her death? Is she waiting for Jeroën?

The silence in the room forces her to think about her family, her friends, Adrian and the tears are flowing like a broken water tap Finally, she cries out loudly, "Jeroën, I don't want to die!"

That doesn't help. All of a sudden, she feels like the oxygen in the room is cut off. She's gasping for air and she knows, deep down, that this was it. She can feel something from within her leave. Flashes of her brother getting a medal at soccer, her getting her first kiss, Adrian getting his car, her dad telling her a bedtime story interrupts her sight. She feels like she's reaching for something. Carmen's gasping louder trying to catch the smallest particle of air and breathe it.

"Jer—" she screams, tears streaming down. She can feel her legs going numb and she prays. She prays for another chance. The light in the room that is lit by the streetlights slowly start to fade out and when she's sure that it was over, a sudden flush of air is pushed into her lungs.

Carmen inhales and exhales wildly, closing her eyes. She clutches the ends of the chair and opens her mouth, inhaling as much as air as she could.

She feels a pair of hands on her thighs.

Frantically, she peels her eyelids open and sees Jeroën kneeling before her. His black hood has fallen off his head and his black hair is distraught. Thunder hits the clouds and Carmen sits up startled. She can feel Jeroën clutch her knees hardly as he yells, "I can't! I can't."

"Jeroën," she breathes loudly. "What's going on?"

He looks up and Carmen can see his grey eyes filled with tears. Sadness looks like a foreign feeling, an absurd feeling on his face. "I can't take your soul away, Carmen. I can't do it."

"What do you mean?"

He cups her cheeks. She feels her cheeks getting warm. "I'm not Death anymore."

"Jeroën . . . I don't get it . . ."

"Carmen!" He stands up and points at the window. "Do you see that?" Another shock of thunder courses through the clouds. "I didn't fucking *meddle* with fate, I *changed* your fate. I didn't take your soul. This changes everything!"

"I . . ."

"With every death begins a new life. One person dies, another is born. It's a circle. I broke the circle."

He paces around the room, running his fingers through his hair. Carmen tries to stand up and wobbles to him. She taps his shoulder and asks softly, "why did you break the circle?"

He stills and in a second, she can feel warm lips planted on hers. Their noses clash and he bites her tongue.

"Ow!"

He pulls back, his cheeks red. "Uh . . . sorry."

"What the hell were you trying to do?!" she snaps, rubbing her bruised lips.

"I was trying to kiss you."

"Why—"

He presses his lips against hers again. This time, it feels good. She felt like was riding some kind of magic carpet over lands of ecstasy and wonder. When he pulls back, she's pulled back into reality.

His forehead is against hers as he whispers, "Because I think I'm in love with you."

•••

Adrian gapes at Carmen.

"You left while I was asleep?" he scowls. "What kind of sick joke is that?"

"Adrian, I'm sorry but I had no choice. Does it really matter now?"

"Yes, it does because—"

"Did you call her?" Jeroën asks interrupting him. Adrian looks at him and stammers, "Y—yeah. She said that she'll be here in half an hour."

"Fine," he says and closes his eyes tightly. Adrian doesn't know how many times he had thanked him and no matter how many times Carmen told him that he loved her, Adrian couldn't believe it. Sheila had told him about the 1500 incident and he can't believe the history's about to repeat itself.

"There's some orange juice in the fridge," Adrian tells Carmen. "Help yourself and there's some pie in there too. You look famished."

Carmen gives him and Jeroën sceptical look but she shrugs and leaves the den. Adrian sits next to Jeroën who's sweating like crazy.

"Do you want me to turn the air conditioner on?"

"No."

"You sure about that?"

"Yes."

Adrian taps his fingers on his knee wondering how he was supposed to frame the question but Jeroën beat him to it.

"You don't have to be so happy, Adrian," Jeroën says tautly.

"What do you mean?"

"I dragged you guys into a problem that's ten times worse than what you'd expect."

"How so?"

"I'll tell you how so." Jeroën leans closer and says, "Carmen *will* die. I have a feeling that we're going to go to Purgatory sometime soon. If Carmen and I do, then you and Sheila will come along. I have a feeling."

"What's going to happen to Carmen?"

"They're going to torture me," he says. Adrian can note a slight shiver in his voice. "They're going to torture me and exhume all feelings from me but that doesn't matter. I don't know what they'll do with Carmen. They'll probably take her soul away or maybe they'll let nature do it."

"What about Sheila?"

"Her father is mad at her. Most likely she won't be sent down to Earth."

"And . . . me . . . ?"

Jeroën smiles a sad smile. "You'll get the worst, I suppose . . . for daring to love the daughter of a supreme being."

• • •

"So," Sheila says, wiping her tears. "We're going to end up in a lot of trouble."

"We know," they say in unison.

"And this will probably be the last time we see each other."

". . . We know."

Sheila opens her fist and holds out three white pills. "They're sleeping pills. I've taken one. You guys will have to take one to. Jeroën, you don't really have to—"

"I want to," he says quickly.

"Okay. Take it and go to sleep. Pretty sure you guys are going to end up in Purgatory when you wake up."

• • •

"Hey Adrian? You in Purgatory yet?"

"No."

"Guys, *sleep!*"

"I don't think the pills work."

"Yeah," yawn, "no, I think it is."

• • •

Chapter 38

Adrian Opens His Eyes to Complete Darkness

He blinks again. Complete darkness. He does it again until he wonders if he's actually blinking. The ground feels cold as he places his hands on the cold floor. He doesn't know how he ended up on the floor and neither does he know where he is.

"Sheila?" he calls out softly.

"Adrian!"

"Carmen, is that you?"

"Yeah! You're here?"

"Yeah, I guess . . . where are they?"

"I don't know. I think it's just us." He hears Carmen sigh. "Where are we?"

"Is this Purgatory?" Adrian asks. "I can't see a bloody thing."

They hear footsteps and suddenly, light floods in that Adrian squints his eyes in pain.

"Get up."

He looks up and sees a bald man in a black suit. He looks intimidating as he stares down at Adrian with his red piercing eyes and it makes him want to crawl and hide.

He stands up, staggering in the process and sees Carmen in the corner of the room. As Adrian looks around the room, he realises that it's a cellar.

"Uh . . . where are we?"

The man raises his thick eyebrows at Adrian's question. "You are in a cellar."

"I *know*. Why are we in a cellar?"

He sighs. "This is a dungeon where souls are kept until they are called for purification."

Carmen gasps and walks closer to Adrian. Adrian looks at how muddy her face is and doesn't want to imagine how he looks right now. "That means we're dead?"

He rolls his eyes. "No. Do not ask me why you are here. You two are the first humans to have stepped into Purgatory without having to encounter death," he smirks slowly, "and for a peculiar case indeed."

They gulp.

"Anyways," he continues, "you have been sent for by Percontator. Line up against the wall."

Carmen and Adrian exchange a petrified look before lining themselves against the wall. The man surveys them, his eyes running up their bodies and Carmen shuffles nervously.

"Follow me."

The man pushes open the door and steps out waiting for the duo to step out as well. When Adrian steps out of the cellar, he's engulfed in sounds of moans and pleas.

Adrian clutches Carmen's hand tightly.

The man leads them down the corridor. There're lanterns that light up the entire corridor. At the end of the corridor, there's a swirling staircase. The man nudges them. "Move along."

They scowl inwardly and walk up the stairs, trudging. Carmen doesn't know why but she feels like she had walked through an entire country.

Adrian trips on a step but he's slapped on his back by the man roughly. He lets out a yelp and turns around to see the man glaring at him in anger. "Can you not walk human?"

He feels useless and worthless under his gaze so he nods mutely and nudges Carmen to walk faster. She fastens her pace and they continue walking upwards.

Finally, when Adrian thinks he's going to pass out by the dizziness in his head, Carmen reaches the end of the staircase which leads to another corridor. This corridor was ignited by lights and they stagger like criminals through the corridor. Adrian looks up and sees people looking at them with accusing looks. There were ladies dressed in velvet gowns and glowing with diamonds that lace their necks and ears.

Carmen hates the looks she's getting. The accusing stares make her feel like a culprit.

The corridor leads them to a large hall. Adrian grasps Carmen's hand tautly as they looks around the hall.

They are captivated by the large chandelier in the middle of the room. The reflection of the gems scatter around the hall and it looks heavenly. They walk further into the hall and they are faced by two looming hooded figures.

Adrian can't help it and he's pretty sure that Carmen can't either because the duo falls to their knees. They bow their heads and he feels like he's not worthy enough to be in front of them. The power that they emanate makes their eyes water.

"The girl is not that fearless after all," one of them chuckle.

"I cannot believe that my daughter fell in love with this puny little human. He cannot look at my eyes."

At this comment, Adrian looks up. His green eyes meet with sparkling red ones who glare at him fury.

"You are Adrian O'Connor?"

". . ."

"*Speak up!*" he yell.

Adrian jolts like an electric shock coursed through him. "Y—yes."

He takes off his hood and Adrian gulps. He has long hair that fall on his shoulders and his teeth are sharply pointed as he grins wickedly at him. There're engravings on his head and he couldn't make out what it was but like the engravings on Jeroën arms, they moved. Words dissolved into his skin and some appeared.

His gaze falls to his hands. Hi nails are long and crooked and Adrian can feel a shiver crawl up his back. He sneaks a look at Carmen who looks transfixed as he is.

"Stand up," he orders.

They do so.

He looks at Carmen and says, "Are you the girl who interfered with fate?"

Carmen gulps and before she could answer, he says, "I'm Iudex: The Judge. This" —he points at the person next to him who looks like his twin except he had golden eyes that gleamed every time he blinked— "is Percontator: The Interrogator. But I assume you already knew that?"

They nod.

Iudex smirks and Adrian feels his jaw tick. "Follow me."

Carmen watches his black cloak drag behind him and it's like watching a snake slither. They follow him out of the hall and into a fleet of stairs. Adrian and Carmen exchange petrified looks.

Iudex and Percontator lead them to a rom. They smirk and push the door open.

Jeroën moans out in pain. He's chained to the wall with his shirt off. There's black smoke emitting from his body and as soon as he sees them, he tries to smile.

Carmen lets out a shriek and Adrian clutches her hand roughly to quieten her. Iudex hears her and turns around with a grin.

"Does this hurt you?" he asks with a grin. He waves his hand and Jeroën wrenches in pain again, a puff of black smoke erupting from his chest.

"Stop it," she whispers.

"Stop what?" He waves his hand again and Jeroën lets out a sharp scream. Carmen can see his shoulders wobble in pain.

"Carmen Collins. Has *Jeroën* ever told you what happens to Deaths who turn human?"

"Please stop torturing him! It's not his fault!" Carmen cries desperately.

"Torturing?" He asks in mock horror. "Whatever do you mean by that?"

"Father!"

Everyone in the room whips their heads towards the door. Sheila stood there with a furious expression.

"Sheila?" Adrian says in happiness. "You're okay!"

"Of course she is okay," snaps Iudex. "She's in her *home.*"

"Leave Jeroën alone!"

"Say another word and you'll be here," he sneers back at her. "You know I won't hesitate."

She purses her lips tightly and falls silent. Iudex turns to Adrian. "You are quite the daring human, aren't you?"

Adrian doesn't respond. Instead, he looks directly at him and doesn't waver one bit.

"I will get on with you after this," he says and clicks his fingers. Jeroën yells out in pain again and hangs his head down in exhaustion.

Percontator shakes his head. "His feelings have not changed. The girl apparently got him good."

"That is why he has not obeyed us! That is why he has let her live!" Iudex walks closer to Jeroën. He trails his nail across Jeroën's abdomen and Jeroën hisses in pain.

"You are not transforming," Iudex says in wonder. "Wow. This is something else. Ah, I know what will help."

He gestures Carmen to come to him but Adrian pulls hr back. "Please don't do anything to her," he pleads. "Please don't."

"Move away!" he roars and waves his hand. Adrian lets go of Carmen and hits the wall before slumping down to the ground.

"Adrian," she whimpers as she walks towards him slowly. He pulls her closer and trails his nail on her neck. "Now, tell me *Jeroën*, what would happen if I slice her neck off?"

"No!" Jeroën yells. "Don't."

Carmen screams as she feels something piercing her neck. In the bag round she can hear Sheila crying. "Stop!" Jeroën cries. "Please stop!"

Percontator slaps him and sneers. "Shut up, you disgrace."

Jeroën chokes and everyone stills as he starts to cough. He coughs and spits out blood.

Iudex whispers a few words and Jeroën starts to yell again. He thrashes around, rattling the chains.

"Stop it! He's turning human!" Percontator bellows.

But Iudex pains no heed. He goes on whispering words until Jeroën's a bleeding mess.

Percontator widens his eyes as Jeroën spitting blood. He sticks his fingers in his mouth and draws it out, rubbing his fingers. He looks at Iudex in shock. "He's bleeding. He not death nor is he an in between! He's completely human!"

"Father, please stop!" Sheila rushes into the room and falls at her father's feet. "This is our fate! You can't take love out of him. He's fallen too hard. I told you, didn't I? You can't stop us from falling in love! I'm human too!" She rips out the skin below her nail and hisses as a bead of blood appears. "See. What are you going to do? Torture us?"

Jeroën looks up, blood dripping from his lips. "She's right. Torturing me makes me porous to pain."

"Shut up!" Iudex yells. "I'll be back soon! Take them to the dungeon"—he points at Carmen and Adrian— "and you" —he points at Sheila— "come with me!"

• • •

"This is some fucked up shit," Adrian mutters, wiping his brow. "This is horrible. What's going on?"

"I don't know," Carmen groans. "God, my head hurts."

"We've been here for an hour!"

"I hope Jeroën's okay," Carmen whimpers.

They heard hurried footsteps and in no time light floods in their cellar. Adrian groans loudly but he feels warm hands on his cheeks. "Sheila?"

"Get up," she smiles. "Up."

So, he does. Carmen stands up as well, helped by a man who Adrian can't recognise. He brushes his black hair away from his face and rubs his defined jaw. "Adrian, you okay?"

"Yeah . . . ?" He looks at Sheila. "Who's that?"

Sheila giggles. "That's Jeroën, dummy."

Adrian gawks. "What?" He looks at the man's arms and they don't have any engravings. "What?"

"Father—I mean, Iudex consulted fate. He can't do anything now. Carmen's fate is apparently written out like this."

"So Jeroën . . ."

"—is not Death anymore. He's human so he's no threat. Fa—Iudex changed his appearance to how Carmen saw him and I'm not his daughter anymore," she sighs. "I'm human now and—"

"So, you had to be tortured?"

"I had to get the power out of me," she sighs. She holds out her palm and in it are four gleaming pebbles. "Take one and rolls it twice. You'll be back in Earth."

"Wait, what?!" Carmen and Adrian shriek in unison. "You won't be coming with us."

"We will dumbasses," Jeroën smirks. He takes a pebble and says, "Make it quick. I don't want to go first."

"Wait, wait," Adrian rushes. "You guys are . . . normal now?"

"Aye."

"You're humans now?"

"Yes, Adrian," snaps Sheila. "Hurry up! We're not allowed to be here."

"Wait! How're you going to be—"

"It's all arranged! Anything's possible for them. I'm a daughter to single mother who lives all the way in South Carolina and Jeroën's dad is a secretary to come kind of established firm."

"Oh. Kay."

"It's all in our head," she mutters pointing to her head. "Take the pebble and roll it before they change their minds."

• • •

"Adrian your butt is on my face!"

"Why are you in my bed? I thought Sheila said that we'd end up in the places we were in before."

"Oopsie."

"Sheila, your foot's in my face!"

"How does it smell?"

"Are you serious right now?"

• • •

And this is the story of two friends who thought that their flaws were the reasons for all the backdrops in their lives. This is the story of them finding their true loves who told them that their flaws defined them for who they are and they would love them wholly for it.

Printed in the United States
By Bookmasters